Published in Great Britain by

L.R. Price Publications Ltd., 2022.

27 Old Gloucester Street,
London,
WC1N 3AX

www.lrpricepublications.com

Cover photography by Engin Akyurt, 2010.
Cover artwork by L.R. Price Publications Ltd, 2022.

ISBN-13: 9781915330130

Maya

Cheryl

Diane Parkinson

Dedicated to my children: Jordon, Jessica, Amelia and Jasmine. No matter how many worlds I create, or how much success my writing garners, you will always be my greatest achievement. I am so very proud of you all.

- Momma xx.

Maya

Cheryl Diane
Parkinson

Prologue

Black people are mad. As the Lord is my witness it's the gospel truth. Just like it's true that 'Duppy know who fi frighten' and 'you can pick an pick until yu pick shit'.

They have different masks for different aspects of their lives in order to function effectively within the white dominated society they find themselves in. They pretend and *be* what is acceptable in that given situation, rather than just be themselves. Some of us pretend to be different people in different situations, confusing ourselves as to which, if any, are our true selves. And those of us who survive, have managed to successfully navigate the minefield that is our life, staying out of mental institutions and moulding our personas into a fully functioning body.

But what if...?

What if these masks were personified into troubled aspects of your fractured personality?

What if you were *unable* to assimilate into a society where you were marginalised, and couldn't mould your personalities successfully into one?

What if you couldn't decipher the problem but knew something was wrong? What if you died having failed to fix it?

And then what if you were born again into a blonde-haired, blue-eyed beauty? What if you then found you had access to the collective memory of The Middle Passage?

What if you were accepted into society with open arms, no longer the marginalised? What if you were suddenly given white privilege?

What if you were loved and accepted unconditionally, despite remembering you were once someone they hated? What if your previous jailers were now your friends?

What if you are blue-eyed Mary, but you're really Momma's Maya?

What if you were on the winning side, but you remember being the enemy?

Would you switch sides?

Would you accept the warming love with open arms, revelling in the glory and ignore what once was a reality for you, but is now someone else's problem?

Would you keep screaming-mad Maya tucked safely away while you flaunted being blue-eyed Mary? What if no one knew and no one would ever find out? Would you?
Could you? What if...?

I am Maya. At least, that is the name Momma gave me, even though she called me Saly. Just like Marie is Grace, Daniel is Jason and Jessica is Rosie. Our names are ours, unless of course they are not. Our faces are ours, unless of course, they are not. And our voices are ours, unless of course, they are not. Our blood is ours, until it is not.
Momma with her Roman nose that blushed at the tip when she drank a little too much rum. Momma whose iron-will endured until aged ninety-eight, in loneliness and an empty three-bedroomed house that she filled with her treasured junk. She, with the

persistent pursed lips and the broken brow. Her crease that never ceased. I was the first to try to smooth it away with my flat, fat fingers. My pink palms forced apart the folds of skin on her brow, but as soon as I let the flabby sides go, they sprang back into place - a constant crease that everyone saw and no one noticed. It was part of her face - that crease. And later, those lips.

I am Maya. Single mother to three beautiful children - although where they are now I do not know. Guilt flows through me like a muddy river, clogging my too-skinny veins.

Nothing is right and I wonder, too late, if it ever was meant to be.

I am Maya. I have a Caribbean sway that segues from life to love to hate; beauty to hard-stoned, immoveable discipline. I love with a vulnerability that gets me hurt again and again and I am hard-nosed, ruthless and cruel. I am hoarse from the blood-curdling screams of terror, as I look out into the real world and I roar with a hurricane in my throat to scare away the monsters **before** they strike, **before** they grow up hating and cursing me and screaming at me and lynching me. **Before** they even realise that they are the monster and I am their enemy. I eat the new babies raw **before** they can take their first breath, squeezing the buds of their future intentions out of their bulging, blood-filled eyes. For **I** am forward thinking. **I** am smart and **I** get them before they get me.

I protect and serve. I preserve and swerve from the vicious beast that in my desperation to avoid - I become.

I am Maya. But when I awake, I find that I am Mary. I have eyes that are a sky-blue colour, flecked with an emerald green. I'm beautiful compared to last time. But I'm ugly. I'm pale and pathetic and static. I am milk when I'm meant to be cayenne. Before, music and rhythm used to tap dance through my veins, shimmy up my spine and my footsteps emitted a snapping sparkle that, even in my dreams, would make others stare in envy as I sashayed and shoe shuffled my way through life - 'an unusual one' my Momma said.

That was before. A long time before, when I was honestly and truly Maya. Even I can see that at thirteen.

I have blonde hair scraped into a high ponytail that swishes back and forth as I walk - and I deliberately swish it. It sounds familiar, but not. It's new, but something about it is old. I know it. It's at the tip of my tongue and refuses to budge.

I like the way it feels around my neck, the top of my back. So light. So soft. So new. I've a splattering of freckles across my ski-slope nose. But my lips still purse like Momma.

I may be Mary, but I am still Maya. I still have my Caribbean sway that I will keep 'til the day I die. Again. That's something I won't part with - not for all the tea in China.

I am Maya. But when I awake, I find that I am Mary. I have eyes that are a sky-blue colour, flecked with an emerald green - have I mentioned that before?

Have I mentioned that before?

1

I am Maya. I know this as I sit on the train and Essex whizzes passed my window. It's 8.10 a.m. and I think I may be late for school. The man next to me flicks his paper and I sneak a peek. JetAwayHolidays. Discounts for the white people to set off to sunnier climes. I don't need no sunny climes - it clashes with my skin. I like the way my breath plumes from my mouth on a cold, frosty morning. I like In The Bleak Midwinter and MidwinterBlood. I like the fog and the frost and the occasional smog. I like it here and want to stay. The cold agrees with me.

My eyes flick to the blur of rusty greens and oranges as it races ahead. Or behind.

Yes, I like it here. This time, I'll try to stay. Clare on the other hand, doesn't. I swear she does the opposite of what I like deliberately. She still shouts at me, even though her voice is quieter in this one. In this one, her voice is smaller. She's muted but still there, sharp, at the edges of my consciousness. She is covered by miles and miles and miles of the vast, bubbling blue. She struggles to reach the surface but doesn't drown. She won't drown - that's her gift and curse. Fate has written it into her blood.

Bobbing silently in her boat I absentmindedly think of pushing her out, tipping her into the deep - a vast nothing that stretches out forever into a cool, creeping black. The darkness frightens me. It grabs at me with its grasping tentacles. There was a time when it'd stick, cling to me and pull me into the suffocating black, and I would sink down and down and drown. Not anymore. Now they bounce and slip off my pure, porcelain, lily-white skin. Don't tell anyone but I don't much like Clare. But I'd never tip her out of that holy, old boat. That's what makes us different.

As I look at my reflection in the train window, my blue eyes sparkle back at me. They are a sky-blue colour, flecked with an emerald green and I know I am beautiful. I can feel it in my bones. It travels with me and makes me *feel*. The opposite of last time. Being beautiful gives me a confidence I didn't have last time. I like it. It is really growing on me - *in* me. 'Humph. Suits you.' I hear Momma in my head, which makes me smile.

On my way to school, kids bump me with their school blazers embroidered with red and green and

black emblems; and their rucksacks and their
swinging keyrings hanging off zips. We rush off the
train, shoving each other, busily trying to get to
school but not really wanting to get there. Girls hoot
and scream in laughter at absolutely nothing much,
and I watch. And walk.

It's October and the weather knows it. I have been
here since September. We moved home. I think. The
mother makes noises but I rarely listen. I am full of
Momma and my Maya and my old life. The father is
even less relevant. They always have been.

When I was a child, it was just me and Momma.
We didn't need anyone else. And later it was me and
my children. We didn't need anyone else. Anything
else is surplus. The father is surplus. The mother
should be more. But she isn't. It doesn't matter. I have
Momma - *had* Momma. This thought makes me a
little sad. Part of me felt that when I left, I would see
her again. I didn't. I just ended up here. She always
said that you fall asleep. Made it sound so peaceful.
After a life full of heartache, you get to go in restful
sleep until the trumpets blow and awaken you for the
final time to greet the Saviour in all his pomp and

ceremony. He'd be there all 'other worldly'. That didn't happen to me.

I step over sloppy, wet leaves that make my toes curl in my dark Clark shoes - decaying carcasses that make my skin crawl. It starts to drizzle. My blue eyes glance up at the sneering, spitting, grey sky to see bulbous clouds stubbornly rolling in. It knows. Halloween is near. I like Halloween. Momma didn't like Halloween. They celebrate it a lot in this country. Kids dress up and go trick-or-treating. Crazes from America reach us here and spread like wildfire and so now, most houses get trussed up like a turkey. The autumnal wind winds around my legs and tickles the back of my knees. I shiver and wish I had put on black, opaque tights instead of long, white socks that, now I look at them, make my legs look longer and whiter than ever. Milk bottle white.

Kids scream loudly as they skip over puddles and bang into each other. I can smell Wotsits. I carry on walking, ignoring them and pretending I don't see. Pretending that I am preoccupied with the most important imaginings in my mind.

And as we reach the school playground, we are a

bit early and so I sit on the wet bench. Luckily, I have on my waterproof mac. Momma always said that it was good to be prepared for every eventuality. Momma's words followed me to places she never imagined. I wonder what she would say if she could see me now. If she could see I was doing it all again. But this time I was going to do it differently. I had to. There was no choice.

"Hey! Mary Fairy!" Michael yells at me. I don't make eye contact. He and Saif are looking at me. Instead, I reach into my rucksack and pull out my book. Miss Williams looked at me oddly when she saw me reading this one in our DEER time, but I like it.

"Maya Angelou?" she asked, with one plucked eyebrow raised and her curious, white face pinched. I said nothing. "Wouldn't you prefer something a little more...?"

She hadn't finished her sentence. I guess she couldn't find the words. I considered lending her some of mine but decided I didn't know her well enough. And besides, she might not give them back. So, keeping my words to myself, I just sat and read, even though I have read this one before when I was... not here, but there. Momma reminded me that I didn't need friends. All I need is a good book.

'You go to school to learn, not to make friends and socialise.' That's what Momma said. Maya was Momma's favourite. Maya was my favourite.

"Hey! Mary Fairy Doughnut!" Michael yells again, this time he gets closer and scoops his shoe in a puddle, slopping water everywhere and splashing my skirt. I flinch. There's a bit of grit that lands on my pleated, grey school skirt. I pretend again.

I pretend he is invisible and that I am cosy and warm and dry. I pretend that the sky doesn't hate me and isn't deliberately hurling globby spit gobs at my face and clothes. Some land in my eyelashes, seeking out my tears but I keep them hidden. I pretend that I don't want Michael or anyone as a friend. I pretend that my book is my best friend and that it will talk to me and keep me company when I have no company. I pretend, I pretend, I pretend. I pretend so much that sometimes I am not sure if I am real or if I am a pretend person. My imaginary friend is in good company.

"Mary Fairy Doughnut, head like a coconut! Don't think like she oughta, got a brain full of coconut water!" His sing-song voice was ringing in my ears and he skips around me momentarily, before losing interest and running off with other Year 8 boys. I watch him go as my breath plumes in cold shudders and my nose runs. I wipe it with the back of my hand and smear a bit of snot, which I wipe on my mac before anyone sees. The silver stream glitters but I don't think anyone will notice. The pattern of his rhyme is off... I should know, I am good at music. Was. Maybe still am. I try to balance the syllables out in my head but give up after a few moments. It's cold. I'm used to thinking in the heat.

My blazer fits well, it's just a little big; enough for me to grow. The mother reckons this is best, even though I wanted bigger to give me enough room to grow. That's what Momma had always done, but this mother is different.

Stupid little fucker! Clare's mutters, barely audible. Must be the distance. *STUPID LITTLE FUCKER!* She shouts at his running form. *It's your head that's full of coconut water you prak! Fuck off back to fucksville!*

That fucking loser town you belong to, you prak!

I don't say anything at first, but then something gets hold of me and I say it out loud, even though I need only think it and she hears.

"It's prick... not prak." *Eh?*

"You say prick, not prak. Fuck off back to fucksville, you prick." *Hmmph. Same difference.*

'Not really,' I think to myself, as I watch Michael dribbling the dirty, white football and long for a real friend that is mine.

I listen to Clare as she continues to holler after him. Her voice distant, like shouting into a pillow as she reels off cusses in his direction. Is it getting louder? I imagine the typed words in *Times New Roman* floating off after him, bobbing in the wind and drizzle. They try to straighten themselves into a sentence but some of the letters don't manage it. They chase after him as he runs through the rain. The letters, big and black at first, shrink as they float away, disappearing the further they drift away from me. Clare feels far away and stretches out farther, she is hitched onto one of the letters and is riding an 'O' bareback, as the rain pelts her tiny form.

Yehaw!

Suddenly, Miss Cheal is on the playground,
blowing her whistle early as the rain comes down with
a vengeance. All the kids are lining up for the first
period - swimming. My heart begins to thump inside
my chest as I think about all that artificial blue. It lies,
pretends it is full of warming sunshine, beckoning you
in like an old friend. You expect to see a warm, butter
glow melting on its shimmering surface but it's cold
like death. My eyes whip round as I search from them.
Perhaps they won't be in school today. Perhaps one or
both had to stay at home, sick. As I stand in line, my
PE bag clutched in my hand, I screw my eyes tightly
shut and imagine her in bed, the thermometer
sticking out. And I think, if I think it hard enough, I
can make it come true. If I imagine the detail of her
bedsheets, her mum's feet coming into the room, her
worried face as her daughter has a life-threatening
condition - no - too serious, I don't want her dead,
just not in school. Flu. Yes, her mum realises she has
flu and decides she needs to stay in bed and get
nursed with some chicken soup. I imagine her leaving
the room and - I am brought abruptly from my

imaginings as I see her chatting with some of the other girls. Her eyes catch mine. She smiles, but even I can recognise it as not friendly. She's the sort of girl everyone seems to love but who is as evil as they come.

I take my position behind another student in the line as my knees begin to tremble slightly. I feel the hot tears prick up at the back of my eyes as I feel more than see the girl walk up behind me and take her place. Her breath whispers on my neck. I close my eyes and try to calm my panicky heart. And remind myself what I know to be true. She is just a girl. Just a teenage girl. She's just Annabel. What's the worst that can happen?

2

We arrive at the pool and I change in the changing
room early and alone, I hope, to avoid the crowds. I
know my white legs are pale and blotchy - like a type
of pinkish cottage creamy cheese, which I will try to
hide as much as I can in my black swimming costume.
I don't want to give Annabel and her entourage any
excuse. Using my thumb, I flick the elasticated
material out of my bum cheek and pull it as far
towards the top of my leg as the material will allow,
just in case it tries to ride up my crack when I don't
notice - *they* would notice. You never appreciate what
you have until it's gone. Momma always said that and
I am finding that it is true. I miss my old legs, my old
life; everything old it seems I miss. I never dreamt I'd
have to do this all again - and certainly not here. No
warm breeze to cool hot tempers and bitter cries. No
hushing of the whispering mango leaves as you
sought out shelter in the playground. No peppermint
ball to sweeten your mood when others poured
soursop juice in your hair to cure your cancer.

I get ready quickly so I don't have to sit with the
other girls for too long. I lead myself out of the

changing rooms and sit on the wooden bench while I nervously await the teacher and the rest of the students. I need to get into the water first, so that the boys, as well as the girls, won't get to see me too much in my costume. I think of those Muslim girls that I have seen on the television, wearing Muslim swimwear that covers their arms and torso, as well as their legs. I could do with one of those. I wonder how easy it would be to order one from eBay. I wonder if it would give them something else to talk about, to tease and taunt me with. But I'd be covered. I'd have been proactive, wouldn't I? I'd be fighting back, kind of. Clare would approve.

The bench is cold as I press my warm legs onto the wood. I feel my flesh stick to it as I try to relax. The mocking water whispers at me and makes faces. Multiple sharp, blue angular cheeks protrude out only to be sucked in on the other side as the liquid glass wobbles back and forth. There's a threat in its nonchalance.

I hear the whistle of Miss Grant as her short, blonde hair bobs past in the white corridor, and so I take that as my signal and get into the water.

The rabble of girls come behind me, bare feet flapping on the tiled floor and voices honking excitedly like a pack of geese, huddled together like one big impenetrable mass in their brightly coloured costumes. Annabel has on a bikini instead of a swimming costume. I tut-tut in my head as I think about saying, if I were brave enough, that most normal people save bikinis for beaches. Thankfully, I timed it well, I'm glad that I don't have to sit next to them - I get into the cold water. I hear the teacher's voice lie to me in my head, like the first time I got into the swimming pool water. 'It's not cold, it's heated. You'll be fine.' The water was cold. It felt cold to the touch; goosebumps erupted on my skin; my teeth chattered as I instinctively sucked in my breath. 'It's *not* cold!' she stressed, as I tentatively tried to lower my hunched-up body into the water. I wonder if her telling the lie again and again would convince my body that it was as warm and blue and friendly as the ocean?

The other girls' splashing as they get in brings my mind back to the present. I know better than to complain to anyone how cold the water is. Although the girls' reactions inform everyone how they feel. Even Annabel howls as she splashes in with her friends. They are having fun jumping around in the pool trying to warm themselves up. Eager to be ignored, I push off to do my warm-up length: the frog. *Bend, open, close. Bend, open, close.* I imagine my legs like the bullfrogs I had seen swimming in the warm river down yonder from Grandma's house. *Bend, open, close. Bend, open, close.*

Water was never my friend. Black was no better than blue - they both hated me at times. I remember the darkness; the deep, plummeting beneath my bare feet as my eyes scanned the bitter void; looking for a bottom that didn't exist. My thudding heart, whacking a warning in my chest, a rhythm I ignored at my peril *thump, thump, thump...* slowing, slowing, slowing. I freeze in the freezing... My mouth painfully becomes a large O as a silent scream erupts into nothing; panicking for air, but the choking water rushes in. Bulging eyes; limbs splaying in slow motion, too panicky to do what comes naturally. Too panicky to do what was taught in happier times. Too panicky to make any kind of coordinating movements. It forgets. And I fall.

I fall through the black, into the vast empty nothingness. My stomach and heart lurches as its ice-cold fingers pull me in. Panic filled the cauliflower crevices in my chest until it boiled over in frothing, bloody bubbles out of my mouth, washed clean by the gentle suffocating kiss of death. A silent emptiness holds me too close in an unwanted embrace as my ears are filled with a wicked glee; stuffed with the sharp liquid black.

The void that fell away at my flapping feet. I remember voices screaming as panic ensues. I remember being frozen with fear as I watch air bubbles leaking from my mouth like a precious string of pearls escaping to the clear blue. Wobbled faces and muffled shouts drift further and further away as I drift deeper into the cold, blue-black ink.

I remember the whites of eyes leap out at me from the dim, as groping desperate hands hang onto my ankles, make a grab at my thighs, clinging claws scrape and slip as we all sink together.

Too many grasping limbs, many limbs, too many, too many, too many grasping limbs.

Many, many screaming, bulging eyes that plead with me for something I cannot give them. I cannot give them. Too many grasping limbs begging for something that I don't have. And they take me down with them. And
We sink...

We sink...
We sink and fade...

Fade...
Fade...

And we are swallowed whole into the black toothless maw-of-a-mouth. Give it a few moments and it's as if we never existed. Give it a few moments and peace will descend. Give it a few moments and there will be laughter again. Give it a few moments and on the surface there won't even be a ripple.

Water is not my friend, no matter how much it might pretend - looking at me with those clear, blue eyes as if butter wouldn't melt.

This time, it's been tamed with bleach and chlorine and concrete walls - but it is still cruel, and yet my ears are still ringing with the panicked whites of pleading eyes. I'm disoriented for a bit and my limbs freeze in the water they tell me is not cold. And

I sink...

I sink...

I sink...

My eyes stare off into the blue that is above me as I sink into this not-cold water, but this time there are no limbs grabbing me, just a red mist as I instinctively look for the string of pearls bobbing through the black to the surface - wishing it was me floating away to the top.

I push my feet down in panic and they awkwardly hit the floor of the pool too quickly. The crunching thud of my toes reverberates as I push through the pain and break through the glass ceiling. And as I do, I notice girls, streaming out of the pool like fleas off a dog in the bath. The great exodus. And I see Annabel, her face lit up with glee. Her blue eyes, sharp and alive.

There are shrill screams and swearing as the girls' faces are screwed up in disgust, while others are laughing hysterically as they gather closer to each other so they can get away from me.

I blink.

My breath shudders to life as I begin to clamber clumsily out of the pool. No one offers me a helping hand as I awaken, weak from my remembering. I haul myself out on the side. Wet warmth running down my leg. Miss Grant strides over, her brow broken like Momma. But there is no concern in her eyes like Momma would have had. Brown eyes mask a look of disgust.

"Mary? Are you ok?"

As soon as she asks, I realise that I feel dizzy and I want to be sick. I retch and my body shudders, but nothing comes up but spit and water. Slowly, I stagger to the wooden bench as Miss Grant holds out a supportive hand that doesn't quite reach but hovers near my shoulder. The girls whisper behind cupped palms. Something warm trickles down my leg. I instinctively look to see what it is and see dark, brown blood dribbling from my inner thigh.

My first thought is that I have cut myself somehow. Feeling quickly for the origin of the blood, I only feel smooth skin and realise that I am not in pain. And then it dawns on me. I'm one of the oldest in my year. It's finally arrived. My monthly visitor that

Momma warned me about all that time ago when I was that age. Blood rushes to my face as well as running down my legs, as it suddenly becomes obvious what has happened. I look into the pool to see the brownish-red still swirling in spirals and I wish, I wish, I wish. A gaping friendly hole yawns deep and black at my feet, and allows me to step down, down, down as the black envelops me in a comforting amnesiac blanket that sucks and strokes my skin with tentacles that gently lull me to sleep.

Instead, I have to endure the embarrassment as hot tears sting my eyes and my white nose tinges red. I run quickly to the changing room, a trail of incriminating red spots following me. A few moments later, Miss Grant is by the cubicle. She silently slips a sanitary towel under the door and I am grateful.

I'm Bloody Mary now. Annabel's brainchild. I think it's quite creative really. Nice and original - I consider shortening it myself to BM. It's been a few weeks but the name has stuck. I feel like some kind of leper, but as Momma always said: there are worse things.

The playground has become colder over the

months and as I sit on the damp wood, watching
Michael and his friend chase after the same dirty,
white ball. I pull out my old friend Maya Angelou who
is battered, but she's still good.

The weather warrants tights. The mother bought
me more of them, thicker winter ones, and left them
on my bed – woolly, grey ones that match the grey
skirt of my uniform. As the whistle is blown, we line
up for class and I notice a new face. I find out that she
is Melanie.

Her small eyes are sunken into her head and her
large nose is spread out over most of her face, taking
up room usually assigned to cheeks. She has a large,
oblong body, with no waist. Pale, bare, skinny sticks
jut out at the bottom of her pleated skirt, with
bulbous calf muscles seemingly stuck on for good
measure. Her lips are big. They looked like sausages
folded in two, rolled over in a permanent scowl. A
knife has scored the middle of the brown flesh to
reveal a pink, watery inner lip.

Kids move around her, careful not to touch. I
wonder if she notices this but then decide that she
does, as she rolls her hands up into her jumper to

keep warm, hugs her body defensively and leans her weight on one foot as if she didn't care. She cares.

In recognition of that stance, I watch and do nothing. She's rather ugly. She has a spattering of freckles on her nose and I notice that they are not as pretty as mine. That knowledge trickles around my head before it vanishes innocuously down my neck and makes my own stance a little more confident. She doesn't have a coat.

In my mind, I offer her mine, but the words don't come alive. Instead, I walk behind her in the queue as we file into registration. I overhear someone say the 'n' word and my heart flames to life in my chest before steady hoof-beats thunder through. A split-second later my face goes beetroot red; my eyes become glazed over and fixed onto the flow of walking students as I try to hide from any cold piercing eyes.

Who the fuck said that? I'll fucking kill them! They had better not be calling me no fuckin' nigger!

I hear Clare but can't concentrate on her far away voice. Were they calling me a nigger? And then I realise that they can't be. I am not black anymore. And I remember. And I am flooded with relief. And I breathe and I breathe and calm myself before I feel the slick oil of guilt sliding into my black heart.

I had forgotten Maya. I had forgotten little Maya and the others. I feel shame at having forgotten as I realise that they must be talking about Melanie.

The new girl who is standing at the back of the line. I see she has brown hair slicked up into a bun - except the bun isn't a bun. Her hair at the end fuzzes out into an afro puff. She is the lightest-skinned black person I have seen in a while. Her face, which is in a permanent scowl, has lips that are curled up into a silent snarl.

I smirk a bit as I imagine creating her freckles by blowing into a brown felt tip and have it splatter permanently onto her face - they are that sporadic. She noticed. Her small, beady eyes, fixed on me, held my gaze threateningly before mouthing 'Bloody Mary...' slowly and deliberately, before her snarl deepens and her glare is fixed. My face flushes purple as I turn away but I can feel her triumphant smirk searing down my neck and I wonder if it leaves a mark. Her footsteps get close to me.

'I heard all about The Parting of the Red Sea...' hot

breath and thick lips close to my ear. Too close. I freeze. She whispers passed like some kind of ghost, brushing past my blonde hair which swishes gently in her wake. Automatically, I reach a hand to wipe any traces of her from my blonde tresses, to reassure myself - I find it's still there, still smooth and probably still glistening like gold and I am grateful. More than that, I am deeply thankful. The horses are back, rhythmically stamping through my chest, and I calm my breathing while not letting go of my gold.

There is something about her though. I know that sooner or later I will probably try to make her my friend, as I watch her curl her hands up in her jumper further and we enter the building then take a seat.

First thing we have is French. I hate French. Mademoiselle Murray welcomes us with an extravagant flurry of her hand. Beads tinkle as she swipes us all in the classroom with a flick of her wrist; her pointed, triangle nose poised high in the air as she looks down upon us, her students. I sit in my usual seat beside my imaginary friend, and then I realise that now, that seat will be Melanie's.

I don't get much done, but no one notices.

Melanie's presence flows off her in droves. She smells funny, different - familiar. Clare is uncharacteristically quiet. The parting of the red sea comment upset me. I try not to think about it because the mere memory brings the heat back to my face. I push it away - thinking cooling thoughts.

I wonder if Clare is sailing away finally on that boat she precariously perches on. Or if she's just decided to watch - like me. I remember the swimming class and my face still flushes despite me not wanting it to, so I crouch as low as I can to my desk and pretend to write French words in my exercise book and I wonder if Annabel sees. My hair flops forward covering my cheeks and I am grateful for my low, thick, sunshine-yellow fringe. But I remember.

'Oh My God! She's getting in the water!'

'Can they even swim though?'

'Yeah, haven't you seen chimps swimming on TV? They are okay at it I think...'

Bend, open, close... Bend, open, close...

'Think that black muck will wash off?'

'Dunno, let's watch... over there though, I ain't staying in here with her! Might rub off.' She sniggers at her own funny, snorting like a horse, and climbs out of the pool. Flanked by four other white girls and one boy, they climb out. But I stay in, pretending. But I'm no good at it in this one. My face is burning and I am hot with embarrassment and shame they don't see, but I pretend I haven't heard.

Bend, open, close... Bend, open, close...

If I pretend well enough, the heat will cool.

Bend, open, close... Bend, open, close...

If I pretend well enough, they'll think they haven't upset me and they'll leave me alone.

Bend, open, close... Bend, open, close...

Think cooling thoughts...

Bend, open, close... Bend, open, close...

I wish I could swim underwater. I never was very good at pretending.

Bend, open, close... Bend, open, close...

In my head I hear Melanie's whisper, 'I know all about your parting of the Red Sea' again, and I flush deep red again and my heart flames to life. A trickle of a tear escapes and skates down my hot face. I roughly wipe it away in anger and toss my beautiful, blonde hair a bit more in my face, as I pretend it doesn't bother me. This time I'm better as defiance takes root. My lies become truth. Mademoiselle Murray flounces passed my desk and I turn to Chapter 3.

The bell shrills at the end of the day and I stuff my pencil case in my bag. Maya Angelou's battered spine stares at me from the dark of my rucksack. I zip it quickly and file out of the classroom, shoulders hunched, eager not to attract attention. It's on the playground that I notice the altercation. I'm nosy I'll admit, so I get closer and listen. It's the new girl Melanie and Michael... I think. A crowd has gathered.

"Look at her lips though, looks like fuckin' caterpillars they're that thick!"

"Bit like your head!" she retaliates. I imagine her face, her lips snarling like a cornered dog. Michael and his friends laugh out loud at her attempt to cuss him out.

"*My* head!? Look at *your* head! You can hardly talk! You call that shitty nest, hair! It's gross! I mean, I bet you've had hairbrushes stuck in that crap it's so wiry! I mean... they just weren't designed to cope with that wiry shit!" I flinch at this one and my hand shoots up reassuringly to my own smooth blonde hair and I am relieved - again, before the guilt slopes in. I step closer so that I can see Melanie's face. She's angry. Her eyes are squinted, almost closed, and her stance is like that of a boxer and I think she might hit him. Her hands are in tight balls as she purses her lips. They squash into a thinner line and her eyes spit fire.

"I'm mixed actually!" she shouts back. "My mum is white!" This sets Michael off into further hysterics.

"You ain't mixed!" Michael howls, sensing his advantage. His brown hair glistening, a wind flaps his side fringe out of his blue eyes. "How can you be mixed with a face like that!? You look like a baboon's bottom!" Stopping to grab his stomach, he laughs harder as the crowd around him erupts with 'ooooooos'. I look at Melanie's face and expect to see tears; instead I see a fire storm blazing in her eyes. Her cheeks drain from blood, threatening an eruption.

"Actually" he began between stifled sobs of laughter, "you probably are mixed... mixed chimp and baboon... that would explain the thick pink lips! Must have got mixed up when you were being formed... your face was meant to be your arse!" He pauses again, roaring with laughter, tears streaming as he struggles to get the words out.

"You're supposed to have that red, lumpy backside but instead you got the red, lumpy lips but they flippin' still look like a backside! God must have made a mistake... 'Oops! My bad!'"

The gathering crowd hooted and guffawed as Michael grew in height and stance as he staggered closer to her, flanked by ever faithful Saif, whose black hair and dark eyes turned into shiny, hard-back, black beetles. Michael puffed out his chest like a silverback gorilla, claiming ownership of the playground, the other kids, the school, the city and the country - and if he could, the world. He faced down the interloper. He was nearly six foot now and Melanie had to look up to him. She was winning just not to shrink in his looming presence.

"God doesn't see colour does he? Which is probably why he made such a colossal MISTAKE with creating you! He forgot that certain colours just don't mix!" More laughter. "Still, you have the kind of face that your mother can love. Only her though - no one else..." It was then that I spotted Anabel in the crowd.

Laughing along with the rest of them.

Melanie's eyes narrowed, her lips were still pursed and her fists formed a round, hard ball as she struck out at his stomach with a force that surprised me. I jerked backwards even though I wasn't anywhere near. It surprised Michael too and he doubles over and shrinks a good inch or two.

"You all right mate?" Saif protectively rushes to his aid and Michael shoves him off roughly. I'm shocked. Michael had grown in their exchange and was clearly a lot bigger than Melanie, but that blow caused him to lose ground and that would surely make him angry. I find my feet are slipping backwards and pulling my bag a bit firmer on my shoulders. My knuckles are white as I clutch the strap and sense trouble.

"You wanna say that again white boy?" A hissing and whistling warning, if ever I heard one, escaped hot from the gap in between her clenched teeth. The threat lingers. Michael is furious and attempts to lash out but is stopped by Saif.

"You gonna hit a girl?" he says, as if instinctively jumping to her defence. Although I sense it's more to defend his friend.

"That ain't no girl!" he retorts, "It's a glorified gorilla!"

Melanie has her fist rolled up, ready for more. Her body is coiled tight like she's about to spring at Michael with a fury he hasn't seen before. Sensing it, he decides that it isn't worth it, makes some excuse disguised as a threat and wanders off with Saif traipsing after him. A teacher approaching is his perfect cover.

When I get home, the mother is in the kitchen again, cooking dinner. The dad is sitting on his lounger watching the television. My stomach growls angrily at me as I sling my bag at the bottom of the stairs and stride into the kitchen.

It's a sterile white, which I like, and has black and white, checked floor tiles; like a chess board. I wonder, if the mother is the queen, and the father is the king... what that makes me? I'm probably a pawn but I have an idea that perhaps I may have been a knight. I suspect I no longer have the energy to jump - easier being a pawn.

The prawns are pink and smothered in a sweet and

sour sauce, bubbling in a saucepan. Mum has done her own version of fried rice, which isn't as good as the foreign takeaway down the road but I pretend it is. I grab a fork and spear the tail-end of a prawn. In my head, I hear someone telling me that sweet and sour sauce isn't really a traditional Chinese food. It was made specifically for the English, but I know enough not to bother to mention it. They don't really care and as the sweet liquid coats my tongue, I realise I don't really care either. The juicy pineapples are the best.

It isn't long before we all are sitting in the sitting room with our dinner on our knees. "Things will start to change soon," he says, as he scoops some rice into a spoon and shovels it into his mouth. I nod, eager to please him. "They come here, take all our jobs.

Six months I've been out of work. I didn't realise how bad it was until I tried to *find* work."

"Don't spill on the floor dear." The mother had noticed rice grains tumble from his animated mouth and the fork that he was waving in the air, onto the carpet. Bella ran over to it and sucked it up without the usual snuffling to see if it was to her taste.

The father is out of work and can't find another job, not because there aren't any but because foreign workers would work for cheaper - apparently.

"I have rent to pay, expenses... a teenage daughter." More sweet and sour prawns are shovelled into his mouth as his fork waves angrily in the air. "Now things will change, just you wait and see."

I just watch the television as they show, again, the events of the year so far: the resignation of the Prime Minister has got the whole country in a fluster, and the appointment of another, a female at that, has caused much confusion. Opinions are bandied around and brandished like weapons as the country is divided. The father is now, like many others, very vocal in his political opinions. I understand a bit. After all, if he could get a job, things would be different. He wouldn't be permanently in front of the television, and we would have more money; perhaps go on holiday or buy a car, or something. Things could and would be better for us.

"The pound, it's dipped, but it will soon recover, you'll see," he says as some sauce dribbles into his fair but bushy moustache. In my head, I see a round, gold pound which has lost its shine, sick in bed, with a white, handlebar moustache and a monocle. Mum feeding it chicken soup. It'll soon recover.

My attention gets turned back to my dinner as I spear another prawn onto my fork and I realise something. It doesn't matter that the sweet and sour sauce was created for the English and isn't at all like the traditional Chinese sauce. The red, gloopy sauce trickles out the side of my mouth and I lick it with the point of my pink tongue. It doesn't matter that it isn't traditionally Chinese, because I like it, it tastes good. And that's enough.

At school the next day I see Melanie again in line up. I feel sorry for her a bit as I remember what happened the day before, but I still don't want to stand next to her. I think she might spear me through the heart. I might not survive and I'm a little nervous of her, so I think of spearing her first.

Then I realise that Michael is still bigger than he was before, strutting around in the playground, pretending not to be aware of Melanie's presence, which betrays that he is acutely aware of Melanie's presence. But when the whistle is blown, he falls in line last and we file in.

For the first time in ages, no one has said anything nasty to me. Everyone, including Annabel, is buzzing with gossip about Michael and Melanie. Maya Angelou stays in my bag. Saif is behind me in the line. I am not called Bloody Mary, or Mary Fairy, or anything. I am ignored, which is a welcomed relief. It doesn't take long to see who has the negative attention now.

I remember that I probably want to be her friend, and stare at her as I try to think of something to say. Melanie keeps her eyes straight until she can't. Her eyes bore angrily into mine as her scowl deepens. She has Momma's crease and I wonder if she sleeps like that.

She sits opposite me in registration and in my head, I smile at her, reach out and shake her hand whilst introducing myself. Clare doesn't say anything. I think she is fading and for this I am glad. Now I don't have her aggression constantly in my ear, I feel a bit calmer; things are calmer.

In my head I say sorry for just watching yesterday,

instead of sticking up for her as I ought to have done, because we are the same, after all. And I think, we are the same on the inside - aren't we? I look down at my white hands and remember my blue eyes with emerald, green flecks - mustn't forget the green flecks. They can be quite beautiful in the right light. We are the same on the inside, even if we are different on the outside, and for once, I wonder. Does it really matter if we are the same on the inside? I am different now. My outside is different. That makes a difference. That makes a big difference.

I notice that the pressure has eased off me a bit and so I decide to ease off a bit on the eagerness to stretch out the hand of friendship. I think I will watch and see what else happens. A bit of gold flashes across my eye as it stings and waters. A strand of my hair is caught on my fair eyelashes. Poking through the guard, it touches the soft surface of my eye and with a brief puff of breath from my pushed-up lips, it is gone. My eyes stop watering. I blink away the excess tears and it's as if it didn't happen - that's a kind of magic.

It's raining outside; it's always raining these days. Fat, grey clouds lumber clumsily across the sky. From where I am sitting, I can see the trees lined around the edge of our concrete oasis. They are nearly bare. Their spindly, knobby arms stretched out open to the sky as if waiting for a hug that won't come. 'They'll wait all winter,' I think to myself, 'and if they are lucky, they might get a dusting of snow, although it's much more likely to be rain, rain and more rain'. The worst season I think is coming. Winter bites. Its harsh breath freezes your blood. White winter is never warm, blue or has black notes riding the air - no treble clef in the distance, sitting on a cloud - no. It is cold and sharp. I remind myself that I don't need no sunny climes. The white winter matches my skin. I blend in. I remind myself that I like the cold. And I want to stay.

3

I am Maya. I know this, no matter how much she shouts in my head. She is me and I am her. Clare and I go together. She is relentless in my head, but I think I have learnt to live with her. She's all I have left. She is what is left over. I remember that, and for that reason alone, she is valued. At least by me. Others have more than just one resident personality within them, so in that respect, I am lucky. I think I inherited her. God knows from where. But she has a temper. She's always had a temper. And for as long as she has been in my head I have known she is Clare, and I am Maya.

I am on the train, mulling over my day at work as usual. It's late. Sometimes I feel like I cannot take any more. When I think of how I am spoken to, I'm lost, and I despair. What would my Momma say? My hand lifts and rubs my broken brow, my permanent crease. I am tired and I am drained. Momma would tell me to stand up for myself. But I don't think I have the energy. Or the guts. Perhaps I am just a coward.

When I was a kid, we used to joke around with each other saying, 'I don't come to school to get verbally abused thank you!' to which I'd retaliate,

'Oh? Where do you normally go then?' And I would burst out laughing at my own joke. Predictable and unfunny. Somehow, that made it funnier. As if knowing what was coming was the joke. The banal sameness of the joke never changed. It was so unfunny, it was funny. The very thought of my childhood days brings a smile to my face. Clare was quieter when I was young. Or maybe I was louder. But she has grown. Like a lovable cancer. I can't keep up with her. She says what I should say but I don't have the strength, and the louder she gets, the more she is right, and it seems, the more I fade away.

Sometimes I think we ought to trade places. I should be on the inside and she can be on the outside. But if that would happen, I know I would truly fade. There's a real danger of me fading now, and her taking over this body of mine. The danger is real. It's so very real but no one sees it coming. And I don't know what to do. The closer the devil gets, the more my life force ebbs away and the more Clare screams. I shrink and she grows. That's the silent agreement we have. I wonder what will happen if I ebb away completely. Who knows? It's unchartered waters... no one comes back to say. But all the stresses of life chip away at middle-aged me. Like water wearing away rock.

Children - you think are innocent, will accept you for who you are. And they do. And they don't. Turns out I do go to school to be verbally abused. Happens on a daily basis in the classroom where I teach. Every day in school, the same thing. Constantly on repeat.

It's later than I wanted it to be. I'm feeling guilty again and I squirm in my seat. I'll be late picking up Milly from the childminder. She's eight and hates it when I am late. The childminder doesn't feed her. But *they* eat. 'They' are the childminder and her boys. She leaves my Milly out. It's for the best, I tell myself. So, she can eat with us. Her family. Clare just cusses in my head as I reel off all the excuses I have for not changing my childcare provider. Besides, Milly is settled.

The department meeting at school went on much longer than I had anticipated and I couldn't just get up and leave. They already think I'm unreliable. I know they do. Ms. Delaney looks at me, through her half-moon glasses, like I was twelve. Jacob sits at the head of the oblong table as if he is master and I am just a lowly teacher. It's ridiculous. 'It's untrue,' is what Clare yells at me. It is all in my head. I smile and say the only thing in my head is her.

I turn to look out of the window and see Essex whizzing by in a blur. It's cold and I shiver. The strained sun forces out a reluctant light. He doesn't want to be here either - probably wishing he could stay on the other side. Like a white tennis ball, it hangs in the white sky.

I look at my reflection and see my locks spilling over my shoulders. My eyes blur as the double shadow shows me as a two-headed monster. The shells stitched into my locks look out of place. I look out of place.

I have only been there once - what Momma called a long holiday, for a year and a half. I was born and bred in London, but the Caribbean calls me sometimes. It's funny; I know that if I was to go there as an adult, I would be lying back and thinking of England. I would be longing for cups of tea and cold frosty mornings and condensation dripping down an overstuffed train window as I struggle to breathe. It's funny what you can get used to. And not so funny what you can't.

The red-headed man beside me is snoring. Maybe he is an investment banker or an insurance broker. He's probably something boring. But maybe he lives a double life as some kind of drag queen. I picture red, ruby lips in between his ruddy beard. His leg jerks out in his sleep and he shudders. The tip of his foot catches my leg and I flinch. It doesn't hurt but I adjust myself so as to create a bit more space between us, which is difficult as the trains were designed for the skinny. Of course.

My mind wanders again as I think about Milly and how tired she must be. Glancing at my watch, I see that it is after 6 p.m. It's dark outside. My reflection becomes clearer as the train lights flick on, turning the view into an impenetrable, black rectangle. There could be all sorts out there that I cannot see. All sorts of monsters. And after I mull over the dangers, I think about what to cook for dinner.

Maya likes spaghetti Bolognese. I always buy the spaghetti called Angel's Hair. It's thinner than the regular pasta and lighter in colour. Maya likes it. Smothered in mincemeat, with a mountain of grated cheese on top.

Milly likes dumplings. Momma was always good at cooking sugar dumplings. Those and salt fish fritters, but Milly isn't fond of salt fish fritters. Her sweet tooth prefers the sugar dumplings or the banana fritters. I should cook some, but guiltily I realise that I am just too tired and so will probably just put a pizza in the oven. Maya and Marcia would have snacked on something by now.

The investment banker snores loudly, his voice catching in his throat as his breath halts like a stumbling train. He jumps again in his sleep. This time his hand flings out involuntarily and jabs me in the side. I jump and Clare bursts to life.

What the fuck is he doing? Oi! Fuckhead! Keep your bloody hands to yourself!

For a moment I wonder if he can hear her because he opens a sleepy, blue eye, looks at me, says nothing but rolls over and continues to sleep soundly.

What the fuck was that all about? Doesn't anyone have any manners? Maya! Tell him for God's sake!

Punch him back!

I don't. I get up quietly and head to the adjacent booth. Clare doesn't know 'white people polite'. It's all double-Dutch to her. I take a seat by the black window as shadows flit and flutter by in the dark outside. I imagine black, webbed, horn-tipped wings on demons silently soaring in the darkness.

Do you mind? What the backfoot raas!

She continued her tirade at him. I cringe as if others can hear Clare and her constant cussing, turning the air blue and heating the cold carriage to a blazing red. I say nothing. I just sit quietly, lying back and thinking of England.

It's another 'screaming' day of Clare's. I can tell as soon as my eyes open in the dark, peering into the black. A fuzzy 5.30 a.m. blinks at me from the side table. My head is pounding. I think she's been screaming all night in there - still reeling about the man on the train. I feel a pull on my limbs as I try to peel myself out of bed. It's hard though and I am heavy. My thoughts are of coffee. And whisky. Momma was always fond of whisky in her tea. Whisky quiets her and my head is pounding - I need to quieten her.

The house is asleep. The windows wheeze as I stumble out of my room with a pounding head. I tap onto the girls' bedroom door. Time for them to get up. Little Maya jumps before moaning gently for me not to shout too loudly. Am I shouting? My head is hurting but I don't think I'm shouting. It's difficult to tell with Clare's constant screaming in my head. Blocking everything else. She shouts about everything and anything.

Sounds like inane babble. Gibberish is her specialty. She's too loud today. I need my coffee and she needs whisky.

I park my car and stop in the shop before the train station for some hot chocolate. It's going to be one of those days. The cashier surprises me, and yet she doesn't. My change, she drops onto the counter and turns away without meeting my eyes.

"Thank you," I mutter, as I scrape the coins off the table, take my hot chocolate and ignore Clare's screams getting more violent. She sounds hysterical.

On the train, her screaming continues. I shut my stinging eyes. I don't need to look in order to see the perfectly tilled fields streaming passed my window with soft, green hills in the background. The early morning mist hovers just above the ground, turning the land into an enchanted, forbidden landscape that I claim. Opening my eyes, I take a shot of the sugary chocolate, breathe and look around.

The newspaper flicks as she reads with her legs crossed. Then there's the familiar snoring Englishman. And me. The sky looks bumpy and the thick evergreens race by. Little picket fences hem in what looks like nothing much at all - no horses, no cows, no sheep... just tilled earth. Maybe they divide the land into half - two sides of the same coin... maybe.

Someone coughs. He reaches up a hand and scratches his short, cropped, greying hair. I see his wedding band on his fat finger and think there's someone in the world that loves that. I momentarily wonder what that would be like, but the thought evaporates with the morning mist across the English hillside.

I teach. I'm happy. I smile. I laugh. Clare screams. I laugh. I smile. I walk with a skip in my step.

I wonder how my Maya is. Milly, Maya and Marcia. My three girls. The future you hope that won't be like the past. 'I'm not so bad, once you get to know me...' but knowing me *is* so bad and so hard and so impossible. How can you expect to know me when *I* don't know me? But that's okay. That's all right. I smile and close my eyes in a long, slow blink. I have some really good versions of me that you can try out. No, really! They're very good. So good they trick me too.

Clare screams, but today... I am locking her down. Today I am in control.

The meeting after school is long. And fun. And I laugh. With those people. And they see. My version. So I'm a version of happy. I'm a competent version. And I put on a show. My version is capable. And I show. My version is likeable. And I show. My version is a version that they like; is a version that they see. And they like what they see. On the outside. Of course. Because no one can see on the inside. It's just too damn dark. But I can feel his wings flapping closer, closer, ever closer - the horn-rimmed, leather-winged demon Mastema. It's dark. And I can't see. And I'm scared.

"I can't see. I can't see! I CAN'T SEE! For fuck's sake! Will someone, *anyone*, turn on the fuckin' light! I'm so bloody sick of the dark!"

I listened as I thought that voice was Clare but it's not. It's me. She's listening to me. Have we switched places? But that hope is extinguished as I realise we have not.

I'm home. And I breathe. And I smooth over the rough edges. I stroke them, stick them down so nothing pokes its head over the parapet. There. That's better.

Milly is hungry so I go into the kitchen and give her a million cuddles because she is crying and crying because she is tired as well and because I am the momma, she can cry and cry and cry with me and I will smooth over her rough edges and make everything all right.

"Everything will be all right," I croon at her. "Everything will be fine." I tell her that I love her to fairyland and back and that's a mighty long way. She goggles in mock surprise and giggles in glee and wriggles and wriggles in sheer happiness when I tickle her under her arms, and that makes me smile and I'm warm.

Clare is still screaming; white noise, so I get a shot of whisky to subdue her and she fades.

My Maya is on her phone. Her thumbs like lightning, flicking urgent messages to the girls that she's spent the whole day with. My Marcia is on her PlayStation. Typical for a twelve year old. She will soon morph into the teenager that Maya is. Always on her phone. Always brooding in her room, and I wonder if she has a 'Clare' like I do. I wonder if Maya junior is the same as me. She has never said. So I let sleeping dogs lie.

Everyone is happy so I trot back to the kitchen in a semi-haze. Or I sashay with my Caribbean sway and open the chest freezer. It sighs as its breath rolls and curls out onto the floor, kissing my feet as if to ingratiate itself with me. It doesn't work. "Give it up," I mutter, "I have to take something from your gut, but I'll try not to rip it. If you let it go, it won't hurt as much."

The chicken and bacon pie is given up with a smooth ease. I'm thankful this time I don't have to chip clasping fingers of ice off and fight for my food.

At bedtime I am cold, even though the heaters are on. My bible is on my bedside table, open at Psalms 23... just in case, Momma used to say. I am cold. Even though I have a double quilt with duck feathers in it and there is nothing wrong with my circulation. My hot water bottle is a godsend. I place it on my neck and its warmth flows through my body. I sigh. Ignoring Clare, still screaming. I drift off into a crowded, black void with the others.

I breathe.

I dream.

I am dreaming.

"Omeros. I know this is a difficult text, but it's also a beautiful one. What was Derek Walcott trying to say? Why did he compare Helen to a panther? Can you tell me the significance of the names in this epic poem? And what about the structure? What does it have to do with Homer? Have you done your homework?" My class is silent as I walk from the back of the classroom to the front. And then it all swirls in Van Gough circles and the students fold in on themselves and melt into one. The brown and black of their uniform blur and their faces change. But I am the same.

"Now, use these phrases to help you with analysis... This suggests, this implies, this is comparable to..."

"Homework. Please can you check Show My Homework online and see the exam practice I have given you? Check through the mark scheme, time yourself and see what you can do in the allocated time."

Then suddenly it is exam time and we have not had time to complete everything we needed to do. My heart is racing and I can feel myself sweating. My hands shake. My breath catches - I can't breathe.

My alarm screams at me as my eyes flick open, as clammy panic still clings to my skin. I'm confused. I am scared. My heart is racing. Milly is curled up beside me, her little hand cupped around my neck. For a moment I don't know who she is. I blink. My vision blurs as I try to settle, feeling like tea in a cup, still swirling. I remember. I was a version. Now I'm different. Now I'm Momma. My hand flies to my nose, to check if it's a Roman one...

I peel her little hand off me to glance at the clock. 5.30 a.m. Time to get up. Time to get up. Time to get up.

And I get up. I know what is coming. It's a joke. But I don't laugh.

4

Essex is a muddy blur from the train. I am continually surprised at the changing landscape. All of the trees are bare now but the evergreens remain. The sky is a sickly grey. The soil, a dull brown and everything looks dead without any memory of summer. The world slumbers and I wonder why we are still awake, working against nature's timetable.

My blue eyes stare back at me, *her* eyes. My eyes. Mary's. But I am Maya inside. Wondering what happened to Milly, my Maya junior, and Marcia. I am a transparent shadow to the skeleton trees flying passed. I shimmer and shiver in the pretend glass as my eyes pierce my image.

Hmm... yu face favour duppy. I ignore Clare's whispers.

Blackbirds fly against the backdrop of grey like black spades in the skies. Reminds me of John Crows. They hover. I shiver and push my blonde hair behind my ear.

At school, the mood is sombre. Everyone just wants it to be over. There's a school disco coming up and I think I want to go. Melanie still doesn't have any friends and although I was going to make friends with her, I decided not to. She's too aggressive. She's always scowling, or sneering at me or someone else. And besides, if she decides to launch her temper on me, I'm no match for her. Even I know that. It'd be a quick kill and all the ground I've made in not being despised would be lost in an instant. I'm going into survival mode, and although I do feel sorry for her, I'm not about to serve myself up on a platter as part of the main meal - hell... I've had enough of being school fodder. It's her turn. She'll have to figure out a way herself. And as I think these words, the slick, black, familiar guilt coils up in the base of my stomach. Maya's guilt in me - Mary. I suppress a retch, take a deep breath, toss my blonde hair and ignore it.

Michael, whenever he calls her, calls her Mal instead of Mel or Melanie. Apparently, it's short for malignant, as in a malignant brain tumour. He calls her crazy because she punched him in his stomach. He smirked when he said it and his eyes lit up like he'd had an epiphany or something. Even I had to admit that she did act like a crazy girl, but there was a reason for it. They provoked her. *He* provoked her. A fact that was conveniently forgotten, but I hadn't forgotten. Although, I must admit, I was beginning to.

That story spread like wildfire around school and although no one is friendly towards her, no one challenges her in quite the same way if they don't want to get a slap. That's one thing everyone, including me, has learnt about her - she's violent. And I won't have a friend who will turn on me if we disagree on anything.

Mal doesn't seem to care that no one likes her. She does her hair in these cornrows with these green and yellow beads at the bottom. It reminds me of something. An idea flutters at my peripheral vision and slips away. The cornrows are neat and remind me of corn, except that they are not yellow, they are a muddy, brown colour. My hair is the colour of corn, not her Angel's Hair. I remember seeing that on a packet of spaghetti when I was shopping. For someone. I think I was buying it for dinner but I can't quite remember.

I wonder if she wants shiny hair like the girl on the shampoo advert. I wonder if she washed it, what it would look like. Probably a frizzy afro bomb. I wonder if she uses the shampoo they advertise on the television.

I watch her when she walks around school; when she sits at her desk, when she tries to talk to a teacher. She bristles. She's sharp. She's dangerous.

She seems permanently angry, or she just shows off. The way she walks sometimes tickles the corners of my mind. I think she's familiar.

She sways like palm trees, she saunters like a cool breeze over the misty morning mountain tops, as if she is so high up that nothing and no one can touch her. And when she talks to a teacher, she shows off. She always knows the answer as if she has some kind of voodoo magic going on. I'll be honest, it gets on my nerves. I'm glad I revised my plans to be her friend. It would be dangerous. I don't understand who this girl is; if at all, she is a normal girl. Something in me tells me that she is not and it would be better for me if I kept away from her.

And something else has happened. Michael has completely stopped calling me names. It happened slowly at first. The name Bloody Mary was shortened to BM very early on, and then once Mal arrived, she took all the negative attention off me and now Clare has silenced. I guess that's the way it works. Before I came it was someone else who got hassled - probably Sophie. I eased things for her with my arrival just as Mal is easing things for me; law of the jungle I suppose.

November rain stings. I wonder about acid rain and how the clouds suck up water that has been tainted, and attempt to recycle, but it comes down as tainted as it went up. Our fault I suppose - mankind. Our fault it stings now.

As I sit in the playground, on my familiar bench, I have no need to take out my book as now the gaggle of girls congregate around me, tongues flapping non-stop. Nothing is said or has been said about their congregating near me but I am allowed to listen in.

Annabel, with her strawberry blonde hair and her orange lip gloss, is applying yet more onto her pale lips. Annabel, Sophie, Elizabeth and Charlotte the shallot (on account of her small stature). The topic of conversation is Mal.

"I mean, why is she even here?"

"To learn of course, it's a school... duh!" Sophie

chides in. I can tell she's the kind of girl that speaks without thinking. Even I knew that that was challenging, making out that Annabel was an idiot - to which she is, but an idiot that I need to make friends with.

Better to have her as a friend than an enemy. I don't say anything, but I listen and silently agree with Sophie. The difference with me was that I was clearly smart enough not to vocalise it.

"Well, of course!" Annabel says, sighing as if to show that she's not stupid. She smooths out her skirt at the back and presses it to her legs as she sits down. "We're all here to learn, but of all the schools to go to, why St Augustine's? Why here? I mean, surely she'd be better off in London where it's more... *multicultural* or something. She'd feel more comfortable. wouldn't she. with people of her own kind?" I examined Annabel out of the corner of my eye. Her strawberry blonde hair was too perfect. Probably came out of a bottle. And her lip gloss was just the right tint of orange to make it look like she just had perfect, naturally tinged lips. Plump, shiny lips, like some kind of fruit. I had guessed it was for the boys.

"I suppose so." Sophie narrowed her eyes and watched Mal sit on the bench opposite us. She's reading. I try to squint to see what it is and my heart leaps when I recognise the author's name. Angelou. My face flushes as I look down into my open bag and immediately zip it up before anyone sees my secret conspirator. I will need to go to the school library and get a new substitute friend... although I am hopeful that perhaps I may not need one.

Saif runs by. Elizabeth wrinkles her nose as she watches him chase the ball. "Think Mum might take us for a chinky tonight..." she says absentmindedly.

"I mean..." Annabel continued, "we're a good school here, and I suppose she seems a bit clever..."

She's brilliant! Clare chorused in from somewhere in my head. She was back. Can't say I missed her. I flinch. I have not heard from her in a while and her presence startles me. Her voice though has changed. She seems even further away. I imagine her on a boat, floating across a vast, blue-green sea. I look inwards and closer. She is shouting but I don't catch all the words she is saying. I close my eyes. The New Times

Roman black, bold words tentatively wobble and float from her mouth, but as they float towards me, a wind blows them away before they reach my ears. I see the small, black shapes wobble in the wind and then float away in the wrong direction. Perhaps it's better that way.

Opening my eyes, I turn towards Mal and she is engrossed in her book, eyes down, legs crossed like an Indian. She's pretending. My face blushes and my body gets hot with embarrassment. I've done the same thing. I push the thought away, far away, like Clare. And like soup, I am taken off the boil.

The bell is going to go any minute and I notice Saif running around looking panicky. Not paying much attention to him or the other boys, I pick up my bag and make my way to Merici building.

"Who you going to the Christmas ball with?" Annabel directs her question at a girl called Reign, who joined the group as they got ready to walk to class. Reign is chubbier than the other girls and not quite as pretty. Her frizzy, brown, tight curls are stuck to her head in only what can be described as an unattractive way. And I am thankful again for my silky, blonde hair. She's grateful to be included within the group because she is fat and her family doesn't have as much money as the rest of us. Not that we are rich, not by a long shot, but we still have nicer houses than her - even I know that. I am prettier than her and wouldn't be surprised if I become more popular than she is, now that Mal has arrived. After all, she has quite a flat nose, more like Mal's than anything else, plus she is fat. I am slim enough with freckles. Freckles count for a lot in this world. In fact, when I think about it, there isn't much that she does have. I turn my head towards Reign.

"Has anyone invited you though?" I say with an eyebrow raised. It's the first time that I speak. Fake it 'til you make it. I'm one of them now. Time to assert my authority. And let's face it, I look better and should be higher than her.

The other girls stop and look at me but I stand my ground. I glare at Reign in such a way that it is *her* that flushes red instead of me. She shifts her weight uncomfortably. Her hand pulls a clump of hair as she tries to force it behind her ear. And the silence stretches out between us as her hair joins us in resistance and springs back tightly to her scalp. Even though most of the girls are looking at me, I decide to steer the attention rather than *be* the attention - I am learning. As are they. After seeing my expectant expression, they soon get over the shock of my voice and mimic me, looking at Reign and her now deep, purple blush.

"Well, no... but to be honest, I'm not entirely sure I can make it..." It works. My heart thumps hard in my chest while I deliberately control my breathing. Steady... calm... in control. It works. Her voice loses power as it begins to dwindle in volume. I see the Arial, thin, black words escape her mouth and fall on the floor, gasping for breath, dying a natural death.

"We might just have a prior engagement... I will have to check." The last few words are barely audible and I can see them on the ground, a couple of them flipping and flapping about pathetically, like fish out of water. I step on them and swivel my foot, grinding them into the dirt, as I walk into the class. Annabel gives Elizabeth a confused look. Elizabeth turns her brown eyes to me through her heavy fringe and I pretend not to notice. I remember I am good at pretending. A smile curls on Annabel's face as she begins to slowly walk behind me followed by Elizabeth and Sophie. And Reign trots behind. I step over her words on the playground. They aren't worth much now they are dead.

"Science now with Mr. Michaels," Annabel informs me. I smile as relief floods through me. Things are changing.

It's finally the end of the day. I don't talk that much to Annabel and company as I don't want to push my luck too much; after all, Rome wasn't built in a day and I am not sailing on a boat. At that thought, fear prickles at the corner of my eyes and I remember that water is not my friend. Angry at my head for the constant reminder, I push away the image of Clare on the boat bobbing on a wide and empty sea, even further into the distance, hitch my rucksack onto my right shoulder and begin to make my way to the train station.

Before I leave the playground though, Mal catches my eye. Her ugly face is scowling, as usual, but Saif is with her. Part of me can't be bothered to watch what is happening and the other half is interested. Clare is interested; I can feel the anticipation in her staccato body movements. She's agitated. She's shuffling. She's annoying. She may be quieter than ever these days, which I see as a good thing. After all, who wants someone constantly yelling in your ear? But she is still there. Her presence is continually felt. Whereas before I never used to mind that much, these days I find it a little... grating, to say the least. No Clare would be better than a quiet Clare, but quiet will have to do for now.

Saif is standing near Mal and although he doesn't say it, I can tell by the way that he is standing that he is wary. Mal on the other hand is, again, perched like some kind of black panther ready to spring. Her claws are sharp and her focused eyes are wild. Even I can see that. We hadn't known her long but she is a fighter all right. I think she might have gotten kicked out of her last school because of fighting or something equally bad.

They're arguing - that much is clear. Her body is ready to spring at Saif and skinny, waif-like Saif, is stubbornly rooted to the spot, but stiff. I can hear

Clare yelling something but I ignore her. Although, I can guess she's yelling something about Mal. I walk closer, pretending that I am doing something else and then turn with my side to them so that I can listen. I am shocked when I hear what Saif says and I suddenly wish I hadn't decided to eavesdrop.

"Why don't you just fuck off back to your country?"

"Really? You're going with that one, are you? Not like I haven't heard that horseshit before!"

My heart leaps to life and is suddenly banging in my chest, adrenalin pumped at record speed through my veins as my breath quickens. I wish I were invisible. I purse my lips and crease my brow. This isn't somewhere I want to be and I don't want to hear. I should not have been so nosy, but now I am here, I am frozen to the spot and I cannot move. I'm scared. I'm literally scared and I want to cry out, but I don't. Clare, however, is blazing as I knew she would. She seems to love all this kind of stuff, whereas I just want a peaceful life. We listen, Clare simmering with anger.

Mal's face looks uglier than ever, contorted with rage. Her head shakes as she shouts back and her beads tinkle as they are thrashed back and forth.

"Yeah, I'm going with that one. You think we are daft? You come here from God knows where with your criminal ways..."

"'*Criminal*'? And '*God knows where*'? How many times do I have to tell you idiots! I was BORN HERE!"

"Well, I'm hardly gonna believe your word! Not unless you can prove it! You're a fuckin' inbred thief and I want my wallet back! All you people do is steal and lie!"

Even I can sense the danger of the situation from where I stand. I shuffle on my feet and slowly, very slowly, begin to edge away. I do not want to be here. The air is tingling. I can see sparks of cold, blue electricity as it is snapping and fizzing before my eyes. I try to force myself to calm down.

You people? What kind of tomfoolfuckery is this? Clare's got her voice back and I can feel her getting stronger. She is closer than before but still far away enough for me to feel okay about it. But my heart sinks. I thought she was going away.

I wonder what Mal is doing and my eyes flash in her direction. She hasn't hit him yet but I can see that she wants to. I turn my eyes away again because the electricity around them is so bright and sharp and snappy that it is dazzling me a bit. I want to run, but I still cannot move. So I tentatively take tiny steps away, while I continue to listen.

"I want my wallet you fuckin' inbred. No, fuck that, you're a fuckin' monkey, that's what you are."

"Oh, how original..." Mal croons at him as if she was bored. "Why don't you just fuck off back to Paki land, you fuckin' Paki."

"Paki land? I was born and bred here mate!"

"Oh! Like me?"

"And yeah, I am original, unlike you, you fuckin' cunt. Look at ya! Call yourself a girl? You're as masculine as they come! Look at those fuckin' elephant tits! You're a fuckin' animal! A fuckin' gorilla! That's what you are! A big, hairy, fuckin' MALE gorilla!" Mal is quiet. So is Clare. The air tingles dangerously. "Someone stole my wallet and I know it was you."

"I did not steal your wallet and I am no thief." Mal's voice is smaller. I can't quite believe it so I turn to see and sure enough, Saif has grown tall and Mal has shrunk.

Fuckin' inbred! Clare yells, as she bobs on her boat a bit closer.

"Call a spade a spade..." he says triumphantly.

"I'm no spade either." Her voice is almost a whisper now.

"I want it back you n-... or else." Even I could tell that that word was just on the tip of his tongue.

Oh! Dare you *say it! DARE you! I'll fuckin' knock you out!* Clare's small boat bobbed furiously, threatening to tip her out into the sea. Her tiny, brown fingers clung onto the edge. I could see her clearly now, she was closer... much closer, and I wonder *when* that happened. I blinked and she was here. Is that all it takes?

"Or else what? What's skinny, little, pathetic Saif gonna do?" Some of Mal's fire was back.

The nearby streetlight buzzes to life casting an eerie, orange glow over the playground. Saif is now bigger than ever and his shadow stretches. I imagine it skinny and long; elongated fingers stretch, reaching out to touch my toes. I shuffle sideways out of their grasp. Looking at him to see if he means his threat, I can see his eyes have gone hard and cold. His hair has flopped in his face, a heavily bobbed hairstyle suddenly makes him look a little dangerous. Unpredictable. Wild.

I *really* don't want to be here and I suppose I could just slope off; I could shuffle off and disappear and they wouldn't notice - but I can't. There's a part of me that must at least witness what is happening. I don't like it but I give in to it anyway. Call it curiosity or nosiness, or some kind of moral conscience - the outcome was the same. Against my better judgement - I was staying. Reluctantly, staying.

"I'll fuckin' knock you out... girl or no girl."

"Thought I was an animal?"

"Shut the fuck up! I don't care how you do it but I want it back! Understand? That plain enough for ya? You understand those kinds of words? Or do I need to spell it out in monosyllables?" He stomps off. Mal, on the other hand, is still there. Then there was nothing.

"Dickhead. Pretty sure you don't know what monosyllables are anyway."

Should I move yet? I wondered. My hesitation committed me to staying that bit longer. I hear her shuffle about a bit and, risking a glance, I take a look.

She is sitting on the wooden bench. For once, her face wasn't screwed up but is deflated, crushed and droopy. My heart sinks. She looks so sad. I can see her shoulders hunched up too close to her neck and then, the unmistakable sniff. She is crying. She's actually crying.

Now is the time that I could go up to her and speak to her, but I imagine it in my head.

I go up to her. Her face hardens as she realises that I was there all along and I just listened and did nothing. She turns her anger on me, her fists screwed up and thumps me in the face.

Perhaps I should have stepped in. I can feel Clare agreeing with this statement. She would've given me the words I needed to say. She would've told me where I needed to stand, and perhaps she would've helped me to grow larger in front of Saif. And I admit, Mal and me against Saif was tempting. But. She wouldn't give me the courage I needed to do that. She wouldn't help me against the girls the next day, when it spread around the school what I did. My imaginary (I want to say friend but that's a bit of a stretch) person, couldn't help me when I needed her. And I realised that I didn't want to help. I just didn't want to. I don't want to get involved. I certainly do not need that aggro when it looks like I have just got rid of being the one that is picked on. It was all over for me. Mal would have to learn to cope, as I did. She will have to figure this one out by herself. Maybe it was kind of like a test of character. And so, I do the only thing I can do now. I slowly and quietly slip my rucksack over my right shoulder and slink away, leaving her on the bench alone and crying under the orange glow of the streetlight.

I do feel sorry for her but I can't get involved. She looks like she can handle herself anyway, especially after punching Michael last time. I don't know why she didn't punch Saif too - I would have. Well, I'd like to think I would have. Every time something happened to me, I didn't fight. I just let it wash over me and then blow over. Which is all the more reason why I could not just throw away my chance like this, by siding with her. That would be such a stupid thing for me to do - and I am not stupid.

I think about what I have just seen as I walk down the cold street to the nearby train station. The journey home suddenly seems long and cold. I should've brought my scarf.

'She could very well have taken his wallet for all I know,' I think as I walk. And I realise that I don't owe Mal anything. Mostly I have seen her be aggressive, argumentative and hostile, truly living up to the 'malignant' nickname. Chances are she did take it, so she probably deserved what she got. The cold makes my nose run and I sniff. In my mind I can see her screwed-up, scowling face and I hope for her sake that she returns the money. Looks like St Augustine lets its doors open to just about anyone these days.

5

I am home from school and it's nearly Christmas. Baubles tinkle on the Christmas tree. Dad still doesn't have a job but it's okay. We have some savings and Grandmother is helping us out a lot. Annabel and I, surprisingly, are friends on Instagram now. I hadn't realised before, but she has a nice side. A sensitive side that I get to see now. I can't believe how much I misjudged her. Everything has been changing since Mal arrived last October and in such a short space of time. Mainly because I have made the most of things, turned things around on my own and I give myself credit for that. But now, as we are getting to the end of the year, I know school will be having a Christmas Ball. This year, things will be different. This year, I am... me.

Michael has asked me to be his date. When I think about it, I think he is quite cute with his floppy hair. He runs his right hand through it every time he talks to me. I think that means he likes me. He also has these very cute hands. Bites his nails so that his skin sort of puffs over the top. It's endearing. Read something like that in a magazine. And he looks at me a little too long, his eyes sparkle ever so slightly, and he looks just a little nervous as he shuffles around - I like it.

Dad sits in his favourite recliner and a hair advert comes on the television. It's one of those adverts where they are promoting organic, natural hair shampoo. The girl is in a beautiful setting. She does remind me a bit of me. She has a similar ski slope nose and her hair is long and blonde, like mine. I wonder if I bought that shampoo, with some curlers, my hair could look like the girl in the adverts. I will try it for the Christmas Ball.

Suddenly it's over and post-Brexit is on the news again. It will take a while to divorce us from the European Union. Divorce takes a long time. I've seen it on television and read it in magazines. When two personalities no longer want to be with each other it can be painful - the ripping apart. I don't much understand the divorcing of a country from a union of countries, but dad thinks we are and will be much better off without the immigrants crippling our social systems like the NHS.

'Didn't the Cameron cuts do that?' Her voice

makes me jump. I haven't heard her in my head for a while... but she's still distant so it's not too bad. I think about whether it would be possible to divorce *her*, and how painful it would be. I don't even know how she got there but, with any luck, she will disappear if I don't pay too much attention to her. She's already a lot quieter. Perhaps she is fading. Finally. Somehow, I don't think divorcing Clare would hurt very much.

Dad says it's better away from the EU because we will have more control over our borders. There's something similar going on in America as well, and the man with the candy floss hair does a lot of shouting as well as pinching his fingers together to emphasise a point. It has nothing to do with me.

I give Dad a peck on his head as he continues to shout at Mum in the kitchen about Britain being great again; how things are set for a change for the better, and I go to my room.

I pass a picture of Mum in the hallway, and for the first time I recognise where I get my sharp, blue eyes from - it's her. Stupid how I haven't seen it before. I stop on the stairs and examine the picture of mum and dad on their wedding day. It makes me smile. I look like a version of mum but I do have dad's nose. It feels good. A warm spot appears in my stomach and spreads and spreads and spreads up my torso to my chest, and then my face. I smile. I belong. It feels nice - familiar, and yet not familiar. Sighing contently, I trot up the stairs to my room, bouncing my blonde curls deliberately as I go. In my room, I grab a brush on my dressing table and begin to detangle.

The *schmoop schmoop* noise of my brush running smoothly though my hair is comforting. I close my eyes and enjoy the bristles on my scalp as it scratches an itch I didn't know was there. The smell from the apple shampoo in the morning swirls around my head and up my nose. I examine the hairbrush and see the golden strands, stranded in the black bristles, held captive - but still beautiful, glistening like Angel's hair. I close my eyes and continue to brush and remember. Momma is standing behind me in the kitchen as I sit on the dining room chair.

There's a mirror perched on the side showing my reflection, while Momma is standing by the electric cooker. My eyes are big and brown; my hair a frizzy, black afro standing proudly from my scalp, splayed out in all directions. My skin, smooth chocolate, is looking through the mirror, through the girl who is looking back at me, like she's me. But she's not. Not anymore. But Momma. Momma is love. Turning towards me, she pushes my head forward with one hand as she uses a heated iron comb with another to straighten the tight curls in my hair. It smokes. The *whoomphf whoompf* fills my ears as with each stroke, smoke puffs from my head like fanned, grey cigarette smoke. Three combs do it and the hot iron comb is put back onto the red rings of the cooker.

Momma then gets the plastic comb and combs through the straightened hair, which now lies down onto the tip of my neck instead of sticking straight upwards. Momma reaches for the Blue Magic pressing oil, scoops some in her left palm and rubs some into a pre-divided patch of hair before gently teasing out more tightly crimped curls. I flinch as it pulls on my scalp; my eyes water. She reaches for the hot, metal comb again, and a *whoompf, whoompf*. More smoke from my pressed hair, and another patch is straightened and lying down.

I had washed my hair previously. Then I had creamed in and combed through some deep conditioner. Momma placed a steam cap on my head for half an hour, and then I washed out the conditioner. Half an hour more of painstakingly blow drying my hair, section by section, before I was ready for Momma to hot comb it for me.

After the hot comb comes the curling tongs; also heated by the cooker. It would take at least half a day to do everything to prepare my hair but there is a house party - and I was determined to go. Jerome had asked me.

He had sent a note through the slit in my locker door. Of course, I said yes before I had asked Momma. When I said, "Momma, may I?" she said with a proud smile,

"Yes, you can."

I already know how the evening will go. We will enjoy ourselves, dancing and twirling and having our picture taken.

When my hair is done, I get dressed. I am wearing a black, sequined dress, fitted but ending just above my knees; Momma wouldn't allow anything shorter. I had on black, painted, kitten heels and my hair was curled tightly with a sparkling hair clip to keep my fringe from blowing out. I hope it won't rain and fuzz out all the hard work.

When I stand at the door, ready to leave with Jerome, there are tears in Momma's eyes. Her Roman nose is red at the tip but not from rum this time. "Maya..." is all she manages to say before her voice breaks, and she gives me a hug. I smile, my white teeth shining through. My smooth, brown skin creamed as I stride out of the door with Jerome on my arm.

I place the brush on my dressing table. My blue eyes, flecked with green, shine back at me. My lips pursed look just like Momma's... in the wrong body. I frown with Momma's broken brow and I am surprised to feel that, overwhelmingly, I am relieved. I'm relieved to be here, which makes me feel a twinge of guilt. I can feel Clare squirm. At least I am beautiful now.

Little Maya has taken to calling me Mother these

days, whereas before it was always Mum. Teenage years can be funny like that. She's pushing boundaries I'm told... by her - discovering who she is. She's not quite a teenager yet but will be soon.

'Mother may I go to a party? Mother, may I have a friend over for dinner?' That's all I seem to get from her these days. 'Mother, may I?' Reminds me of the game we used to play as kids.

I am on the train, thinking about what kind of a mother I am; if I am as good as Momma was for me. It's nearly Christmas Eve which is loved by all of us. School breaks up later and later every year. And there is no snow anymore like there used to be when I was a kid. I remember when there was snow it was deep. I'm tempted to say 'crisp and even', but that's someone else's memory.

All I see now when I peer out of the window is rain. It plops down in great, big, heavy globules. The train is squashed as usual. On days like these, it seems more overcrowded. I struggle to get a car park space at the train station, but today I am lucky. Today my silver bug can sit in the white square for hours on end and await my return. She'll purr a little too roughly when I wake her up on my return - happy to see me. But until then, she'll wait, and freeze, and maybe get wet in the rain. I'll make it up to her.

A man is standing very close to me. His breath flows down my hair and coat. 'Mother may I take two steps back...' echoes in my head.

'No, you may not...'

There's no room to move, no room to breathe. In my heart I call Momma. I just want to collapse and sleep. I think of asking permission from Momma. Momma may I go to sleep and not wake up? Momma may I just get off the train, go back home and go to bed? Momma may I just stop all this now? Momma may I stop this train? I want to get off.

My eyes flit to the emergency handle painted red. Would this count as an emergency? '911, what's your emergency?'

'I need to go home. Right away. So, I can go to bed and sleep.' Except it's not 911, but 999. Everything seems Americanised. More problems.

Not surprisingly, Momma doesn't answer. But I can feel Clare bristling with anger. I know what it is she would have me do, and it's just not in me.

'Oh, for God's sake! Haven't you got a toothbrush!?'
she yells. The passenger's stale breath flows in my
direction - Clare has had enough of it. The smell of his
breakfast mingled with cigarettes and coffee is
overpowering. I hold my breath. Realising I can't hold
it for long, I take a slow, deep, breath in and breathe
out slowly and surely, making it last as long as I
possibly can. My heart slows a little before flaming up,
harder than ever, in my chest as I release. I still find
myself having to breathe in his breath though, no
matter how I crane my neck to the left.

'Sweet Jesus may God have mercy on my soul!
More tomfoolfuckery *shit* we have to put up with!'

Clare's religious cusses are coming out now.
Reminds me of Momma. There is no room to move, to
breathe, to even shift a tiny bit, and so I endure both
the bad breath and Clare's cusses until it is my stop.

I arrive in London in the pouring rain. I am tired
and don't really want to face another day of work and
pretence. It is getting harder and harder these days,
and I could really do with a reset. A long one. It isn't
until I am crossing a road that I imagine the green
man isn't green but red. He waves me on in a friendly

tone and I step out anyway.

An enormous lorry comes out of nowhere and strikes me hard on my side, knocking me sideways. Time slows down. I soar through the air over a short distance and slam into the lamp post. My skull cracks like a coconut and I lose consciousness as the jelly seeps.

I then wake up in hospital and I am glad because I am in a bed and there isn't anything I can do but rest. This seems like bliss as I smile inwardly to myself and I wish. 'Momma, may I?' I ask hopefully, and I hear Clare's voice, stubbornly ring in my ears...

'No, you may not'.

Instead, I step gingerly over the wet puddles and the dog shit someone else has smeared into the concrete and walk calmly to work.

The day finishes swiftly and I soon find myself back on the platform, going home. I say it finished swiftly, but I can't really remember. These days, I have time disappearing. God knows where, but I don't seem to be messing anything up so that's a blessing. I just wake up in places with no recollection of how I got there. I think I just sort of switch on autopilot.

Today was one of those days. I managed to get through the whole day without any recollection of what I did, what I said or where I went. And here I am, on the platform.

I remembered the rain as it fell, like fat droplets onto my face and eyelashes. It's refreshing. And as I stand there, I cannot help but overhear the train guards discussing women. I am as quiet as a mouse, like I always am, and I listen. A tall, young, black man with a brittle beard and young, sprightly eyes who is speaking to another, shorter fair- skinned man.

"Nah, man... I'm just not interested in them y'know."

"Yeah man. I get ya. Some light-skinned ones are all right but generally, they're a much tougher crowd."

"Don't you like any of them though, bruv?"

"Not really you know. Lots of them are just too aggressive. They give you a hard time. Don't you think?"

"Yeah, bruv. I know exactly what you mean. Besides the fact, I just ain't really attracted to all that. It's all right on tele an' all that but in real life?" He shook his head.

"Just naturally pulled towards other girls innit?"

"Yeah man. I dunno."

Eh? What's this? Clare was getting started. *What kind of new-fangled fuckery is this!?* I sigh inwardly and wish I could just shuffle away. *He don't like black girls! Is that what this prat is saying? Oi! So, yu mudda na black? Hmm? Yu too good fi de black g'yal dem hm?'* Clare was now coming out with the Jamaican. I decided that I needed to get away from these two fools immediately, but it wasn't that easy. The train doors would open right where I was. I couldn't move and risk not getting a seat.

"You wiv a girl now thou'?"

"Nah, not at the moment, but I'm kinda lookin', know what I'm saying?" He chuckled, as if speaking code for something else. The shorter one tipped his hat to one side and glanced down the track for the oncoming train.

No decent black girl would put up with your arse! Yu face favour bomboclaut! Sometimes, Clare just goes too far, and I feel my face get hot. If I was white, I'd be red.

"What about you?"

"Yeah man, been with my girl a few months now. It's all good. She's a blue-eyed beauty, you get me?" They chuckled together as the larger one had an idea. I can see it literally crawling across his face and could guess it before he managed to utter a single word.

"She got any sisters mate?" He guffawed loudly which I thought sounded a lot like the braying of a donkey, to which the other joined him in what I supposed was laughing.

Would love to see the black woman who would put up with those fuckin' fools! Clare says, this time in a normal voice instead of shouting, and for once, I agreed.

I think I have lost my Caribbean sway. Which is just as well. I'm beginning to really fit in now and don't want anything to mess it up and get me negative attention. Going to school, things have changed, but I still remember. Sometimes the guilt is an oil slick curled in the pit of my stomach, other times, it is as if it never was there. Mal makes me feel guilty and at times I hate her for it. It's gotten so bad that most of the time I can't stand to look at her ugly face. It makes me wonder about her mum, who's supposedly normal. What on earth did she see in Mal's dad? I'm assuming that Mal looks like her dad and not her mum. Out of curiosity, I'd love to see what they both look like.

Mal has been at school a while now and she's still as unpopular as ever. The last I saw of her was an argument she was having with Saif in the school playground. As I sit on the bench, I think of what was said and convince myself that I had no other choice but to do what I did. She probably did steal that money anyway. I wasn't about to tell Annabel and Sophia about it though. All I can think about is the Christmas Ball.

"Mal got rubber lips 'cos her momma give her hot chip!" This time I don't even glance round in their direction, or see who it is who is picking on Mal. I'm sure she is giving as good as she gets - she's good at that. She's big enough and ugly enough to take care of herself.

"So, what are you wearing to the Ball? John is taking me." Annabel blushed at this revelation, but I could see that it was something that she was desperate to brag about. Reign sat mute next to me and listened. Her wide, watery eyes looking admiringly at Annabel as she lapped up everything she had to say. She reminded me of a fat dormouse looking at a hunk of cheese it wanted to eat.

John is a year older than us, fourteen going on fifteen. He is strong, muscular, with jet black hair and large, brown eyes. His movie star looks have earned him quite a reputation at school, and even I am jealous. Sophia gasps out loud and I sense that it is more than jealousy of John taking Annabel. I bet she doesn't even have a partner.

"Anyone asked you yet, Soph?"

I have promoted myself to calling her Soph now and no one has objected. Although this self-promotion business is not as difficult as it sounds. I realise that it's a dog-eat-dog world, and you either are a leader or you are led. I am tired of being led, and now, I lead. Besides the fact, I look like a leader. I lead and they are following. It was easy enough. I just stopped acting like a victim and it all began to fall in place. Now, I can't imagine being as weak as I was when I started the year. It's only been a couple of short months, but I am already on the up and up. School can be weird like that.

Michael has already asked me to the Ball, and I have said yes - of course. One of the reasons why I was able to jump the popularity ladder is because I am quite pretty. I've always known it but now I see it more than ever. And, most importantly, I am not fat, whereas poor old Reign is turning into quite the little porker. I am going to the library at lunch and I offer to get her a diet book to help her out a bit. She doesn't say anything but flushes a deep purple, and I smirk to myself and feel myself grow a little taller.

That's the way you have to do it, to grow. You need to stand tall and do what you need to do to grow tall and strong. I am learning. I am learning pretty quickly, but then again I am like that. My brain is sharp - everyone tells me so.

My resolve shakes just a little when I glance back at Mal who is now standing alone in the playground, leaning up against the wall, reading her Maya Angelou book and I am reminded of Maya. And Momma. But I push them away. I push Clare on her pea green boat, further out to sea. I whisper in my head 'Momma May I?', and even though I hear her shout in the distance, 'No! you may not!', I tell myself that I can't hear her, and I close my eyes and force Maya, Momma and Clare as far away from me as I possibly can. I am white. They are not my family and I do not have to listen to any of them.

After all, Momma isn't my real mother.

6

I am ready. Mum and I went shopping yesterday. It was kind of a double celebration. Dad finally has a job and we're all excited about it. Just in time for Christmas. I don't ask what it is because I'm a little too scared to if I'm honest. I don't want to know. As long as he has something and the mood is happy, that's all that really bothers me.

Mum and I bought the dress I'm wearing now. I had taken a picture and put it on Instagram: a little taster, but not too much. I couldn't think of a catchy title, so I left it blank. I'll have to think of something though. All this is new to me, but my 'fans' don't need to know that. I already have over two hundred followers. Annabel helped. Even though she doesn't know she helped. I just helped myself to all that were on her friend list - very handy.

Mum says it looks more like a wedding dress, but what does she know? She's practically ancient now. I'm supposed to be a younger, better version of her, not an imitation. I told her that I wanted it and she bought it. Now I stand and look at myself in the full-length mirror. I slewed it open and reminded myself of Miss Havisham, two versions of me but both good.

It's figure hugging, white of course, and has sequins all over it. A plunging neckline that mum thinks I am too young for, but I insisted, and a fish tail towards the bottom. I think I look great, even though I can kind of see what mum means. I don't have enough of a bust to fill it, but it still makes me look like one of those old-fashioned movie stars. Very Audrey Hepburn. I want to seriously impress Michael.

I toy with the idea of mentioning the Mary Fairy incident, and maybe the Bloody Mary one now, just to see how he reacts. Part of me wants to say to him, 'Look at me now! Don't you feel sorry you tormented me?' Now I am strong enough to say something about how he made me feel. And I bet he's sorry for being so horrible to me; now he knows me better, but I decide not to. It will ruin the mood. I decide, instead, to look beautiful and take pleasure in him trailing after me all evening.

Annabel and I have been Snapchatting each other all day. One of the topics of conversation was the Malignant One... Mal. I wondered if she was going to show up and, if she was, what she would be wearing.

We Snapchatted each other pictures of outrageous African outfits and decided which would suit her best. It was hilarious. Even if I do feel a little sorry for her - but I kept that to myself. Mal brought it on herself anyway. Annabel joked that Saif should ask her to the ball - if he hadn't already. Wouldn't that be sweet?

The white Rococo clock chimes downstairs. My eyes flick to my watch and see that it is time. Michael should be here to pick me up soon. He will be arriving with Annabel and John and we are all travelling together in John's dad shiny, black Audi. Annabel and I, although we wanted the car, were a bit sceptical about John's dad, but John says he's just playing chauffeur for the night and will not chat to us much.

I slip on my golden stilettos and grab my little, gold clutch bag. My hair swishes and bounces to my shoulders - it has grown and is silky smooth. Make-up done beautifully, a quick spray of perfume in the air in front of me that I walk into, making the spray land delicately on my body, and I am ready. I have just enough time for a selfie before I go downstairs and wait.

It takes me a while, but I manage to pose just right

by my dressing table mirror to create a doubling effect. I also change the background with an app on my phone. Now the background is bluey-green, which makes my eyes literally pop out. One final thing and my picture is perfect. I use an app to airbrush it slightly and give me a little, golden glow. Tiny fake tan. A little voice inside me smiles at the irony. I push it away. It's not the same at all.

No one will notice my mild tan, but they will notice I look great. My skin in the picture glows warm. I save it in a folder on my phone, to post later with a few other selected pictures. Right on cue, the doorbell chimes and I gracefully walk downstairs.

Dad has got out of his chair to open the door instead of mum, so I know he is feeling better about things. He seems to have also lost weight, but as I think it, I realise that it's just wishful thinking, his stomach is still a little chubby, which grosses me out a bit. Plus, his hair is receding - double gross. I hope that his head doesn't sweat in front of my friends. I hope that Michael and Annabel don't have to look at him.

When he sees me coming downstairs, he stops and

gives a little gasp. I smile shyly. Mum comes flip-flopping in from the dining room and she also gasps and smiles proudly at me. Little butterflies flutter in my chest. They help me glide gracefully down the rest of the steps as mum joins dad's side, dishcloth in her hands. They seem to have both forgotten about the door.

"My little Mary. You look absolutely stunning!" I beam at him. "Just like your mother!" Here is where my smile falters a little. I look nowhere near as old as she is. That's the worst thing he could have said. My face drops slightly as I swish past them, dismissive of the comment, and open the door.

And there is Michael. He looks pretty good. His hair has been styled and flops lazily to one side, and he is wearing a very sharp, black suit. I smile. He looks perfect and reacts the right way when he sees me. His face lights up. He doesn't tell me I'm beautiful, like he is supposed to, and that makes me annoyed a little bit, but there's time for that.

The Ball is exactly that, a Ball in a beautifully hired hall, but we are sitting down to a three-course meal before we dance the night away.

I hope there is alcohol. Michael reaches out his hand to mine, "Madame?" I smile. That's the correct response to greeting a lady. I clasp his hand as he leads me down our front doorsteps, onto the gravel driveway and to the awaiting car.

I see Annabel and John in the back of the Audi. Accidentally on purpose, forgetting to say goodbye to my parents, I hope that Michael keeps his attention on me rather than Dad, his fat belly, receding hairline and Mum in her flip flops. I glance backwards and cringe as I realise she is still clutching the dishcloth.

When I am seated and Michael, like a true gentleman, shuts the door behind me, goose bumps appear on my arms, but I am no way wearing a shawl to cover up the gorgeousness of this dress.

As we circle the car on the driveway, the tyres crunch loudly and I press the button to slide the electric windows down while I pop my hand out and wave goodbye to the couple standing in the doorway with tears in their eyes.

Something tickles at the back of my brain, but I don't quite remember.

Jerome and I are an item. He says he likes the curve of my spine in my Christmas dress. My face gets hot, especially as I think of what my momma would say. Although, some things are not for Momma. Some things are just for me.

We go out for the evening in a car - we double date. Momma has agreed and has let me date now. After all, I am fifteen, nearly sixteen. I'm practically grown. Jerome is seventeen now, but his brother is twenty with his own car and a girlfriend. Tyrone and Macy.

Macy is at university, she's studying engineering, which I think is unusual and great. She's good at it and she says she enjoys it. Tyrone jokes with her that it's no job for a woman, which sounds so old fashioned that we know he has to be joking. Those days went out with Momma's generation. These days, women can do whatever they want. We don't even need to prove it, it just is. Macy is your modern, enlightened, black woman - what I would love to be like in a few years. Opinionated, educated and confident. Her black-rimmed, very fashionable glasses are balanced on her button nose, her heart-shaped face smiles warmly as Tyrone jokes with her whilst slapping her thigh a little too hard. They both laugh at their own joke, in their own private world in the front seats a million miles away.

She has on a red, tartan mini skirt and a black sparkly, strappy top. Her toned arms are covered with a black, crocheted, fitted cardigan.

We drive down the main road, off to a house party in Tyrone's Fiesta. I'm in the back with Jerome while he caresses my hand gently. Butterflies tickle the inside of my tummy and I have to take a deep breath to steady my nerves. He smiles, as if he knows what I am thinking, and his thumb gently strokes my forefinger. My heart thumps in my chest as I have to take another deep breath. He notices and chuckles gently.

His eyes remind me of the night sky; they shine like diamonds and every time I look into them, my heart just leaps... my stomach starts flipping and when he kisses me? Well, the whole word comes to a standstill. Now that's something I cannot tell my momma!

The road is fairly busy. Streetlights shine above us

as Macy and Tyrone chatter about nothing in particular. I wonder how long they have been together and whether it will last. It does make me think of Papa, and what happened with him and Momma.

That is something that is not talked about in our household. Where Papa is. I think he left us when I was small, but I can't be certain.

One day, when Momma was at work, I did go searching through the top of her wardrobe and although I didn't find what I was hoping for, which was letters from my Papa, I did find an old wedding album. They looked so happy.

Momma wasn't much older than I am now. She looked about seventeen. Her hair was pressed neatly and a curled fringe sprang up to the top of her forehead. And her smile? It was wide, and welcome and young... and full of hope. A beautiful picture which made me sad. Made me wonder what on earth happened that changed her.

Papa was handsome of course, in a smart, black suit, short, cropped, black afro with shiny, black shoes - pointed toes. His leg was jutted forward at an angle, making him look like an old movie star. Where Momma had on a lacy, white dress, Papa just wore a simple, black suit.

In another picture a black Stetson hat perched on his head at an angle and he smiled without showing his teeth. The old photo tinged brown. It seemed a lifetime ago. Maybe even an alternate universe. Maybe this wasn't really Momma after all; after all, Momma doesn't smile like that, Momma has a broken brow and Momma definitely doesn't hold hands with any men. Momma is... Momma. This clearly is someone else.

At the back of the album there were pictures of their first year together, their first Christmas as well as Momma being pregnant. Their happiness shone through like a time capsule. I didn't know what happened to Momma and Papa, but I was determined that it wasn't going to happen with Jerome and I, or whoever I decided to settle with. We were going to be a family: a proper family. I would make sure of it.

Just as I am lost in my thoughts, I realise that the car's chatter has fallen silent. The inside of the car is lit up with a sickly, flashing, neon, blue light and I realise that the police are pulling us over. I stiffen. I can feel Jerome's grasp of my hand getting tighter as he too stiffens and watches the police officer with his baton, slowly get out of his car, adjust his hat and stroll towards us in a deliberate fashion.

My eyes grow wide and I wait, trying to calm my thumping heart. If I was the officer, I'd take one look at my face and think I look guilty. So I close my eyes and try to calm down, muttering to myself over and over, 'I haven't done anything wrong, I haven't done anything wrong'. It doesn't work though as my whole body is flooded with a guilt and nervousness I don't understand.

"Don't worry..." Tyrone reassures us, "we have done nothing wrong. It'll be fine." His parents taught him that line too. He doesn't see but I notice him flash a worried look at Macy and she glared back at him; eyebrows furrowed.

Annabel looks nice in her pink dress. It wouldn't be my choice, too puffy at the bottom, sort of clashes with her hair colour but she looks good in it. I thought, from what Annabel had been saying, that

John was really into her, but from what I see he's distracted. He doesn't really seem to be bothered whether she's there or not. I wonder why he bothered to take her, but then Annabel loops her arm in mine excitedly as we recline in the leather interior. I am sandwiched between Michael and Annabel while John sits in the front seat with his dad. Michael casts a nervous glance or two my way and I smile to myself with my cherry pink blush lips. It not only smells of cherry but as I run my tongue along my lips, it tastes of cherry too. Turning to Annabel, I tell her how fantastic she looks, and she gushes.

"But you look absolutely stunning!" she says. I smile and offer my thanks, and I must say that I think she is right. I hope Michael heard. I'm one of the oldest in my year and at thirteen already, I consider myself to be a teenager. So where I am thirteen, Annabel is still only twelve. This makes me better. I smile again to myself as I feel more mature and feel myself growing in height and importance. I make a mental note to take a picture of myself with John and his car, as well as Annabel, so that I look more sophisticated next to her. Although I do not have a full woman's figure, it is getting there. I have a waist and a nearly-bust, whereas Anna is straight. In her pink, fluffy dress, she looks closer to ten than a teenager.

Her little clasp bag is like mine, except she has a pink, glass-beaded chain attached to it so she can hang it over her shoulder. She may as well have Mickey Mouse plastered on the side. I internally roll my eyes and realise that it really is just a matter of time before I am more popular than she is.

The car speeds along at a good pace as we drive to a more secluded area. Out of the window, the night lights of the town blur into each other as the noise of traffic fills my ears.

The party is on a boat on the River Thames, so it will take us a while to get there. One of the reasons Mum and Dad liked John's dad driving - it meant they could bring us safely back home and he could act as a chaperone. I know it's Mum's idea. It annoys me so much how she treats me like a child, but, I am so excited about the Ball, right now I don't care too much.

The streetlights glare in on us, casting running

shadows over our sparkly dresses and set the car in an orange glow. The window is cracked open a little and I am cold and I wait for Michael to offer me his jacket or something... Instead he tries to hold my hand. I think about not letting him, but I change my mind. I like it much better when he is being nice to me rather than not. When he holds my hand, his face lights up like central London. It's actually so cute that I smile back; a genuine one this time, not a fake one. I'm glad I decided not to mention the Fairy Mary fiasco. It was ages ago and clearly Michael has matured and changed. As have I. My mind flits nervously towards Clare but I find that she is not there. Well, she is, but she is a tiny dot on the horizon. I look inward and her boat is still there, bobbing away on the sea, but she's too far away for me to hear her. I can feel her though and she can feel me. I squint. Yep, she's yelling something. I can see the New Times Roman letters floating above her head. They are too small to make out, but I can tell she's swearing as there are a few exclamation marks, some asterisks and a dollar sign - that's new. She's cussing something rotten, but I am so happy I can burst. I can't hear her and I don't care what she's saying - nothing to do with me.

I look fabulous in my dress. I'm speeding towards London, which is all a blur, in a flashy, black car and I look better than Annabel, the most popular girl in our class.

Things couldn't get any better, so I don't know why she's yelling so much. But I turn away from her and concentrate on the now. Michael's hand is getting a bit warm and clammy, but he still hangs on, so I let him. We wind the window down further and whoop as the cold air whips up our hair and makes our eyes stream. I swear John's dad puts his foot down as we screech down a black road flanked by other shiny cars.

It's then that we see a police car, flashing the blue lights behind us. I turn around and watch as they drive slowly, looking at us in our car. John's dad has slowed down. I wonder if he is going to stop. He doesn't but he turns to face the driver of the police car.

Two officers look at us as we drive alongside each other. One has chubby cheeks, small narrow eyes that are slanted upwards, and the other is thinner and

more looks more approachable. He winds down his
window to get a better look at us. In turn, he gives us
a quick glance as a sort of appraisal before nodding
his greeting to John's father driving and then driving
off and leaving us alone. As they drive off, they switch
the blue flashing lights off and continue at a normal
pace. John's dad glances at us in the back through the
rear view mirror and flashes us a warm and
charismatic smile.

We are pulled over. Jerome squeezes my hand as
Tyron winds down his window to the approaching
officer. His eyes narrow as he watched the dark figure
approaching the car, his weapon secured to his belt.
He removed his hat and bent down to eye level,
glancing into the car and at the back at me and
Jerome. Turning his attention back to Tyrone, he
addressed him.

"Sir, would you mind switching your engine off,
and can I see your driving license?" Tyrone does as he
is told, switches off the engine, takes out his driving
license from his wallet and hands it to the officer. I
can tell by the way he looks at Macy that he is

worried. Macy scowls at the police officers as they approach, one on each side of our car.

"Can I confirm that none of you have any narcotics or firearms in this car?"

"What kind of question is that?" Macy asked incredulously. "We're just going to a Christmas party! That's all!" Tyrone flashed her a warning look which immediately silences her.

"Ma'am, would you mind stepping out of the car please?" Too late. His face was cold and stern as he faked a nonchalant manner.

"What's wrong officer?" Tyrone piped up, "Is there a problem here?"

"Just step out of the car please."

Macy purses her lips together to stop anything else slipping out. Her brow creases, revealing her annoyance and fear - but they don't notice. The officer on the other side motions for Tyrone to get out as well, which he does. I can see his t-shirt damp where he is sweating, and his blue jeans cling a little to his thighs. It's dark. And chilly. Jerome and I are also asked to climb out of the car as well, to which we do. The night air dives into my lungs and sits on my chest. I hear Momma telling me that being in the night air makes you ill. I stand there, my arms around my middle to keep in the warmth as I watch eyes drive passed us, watching the spectacle. And I feel guilty. And embarrassed. And then Clare starts inside my head.

Oh! De police! Is wa yu waant? Hmm? Yu fi trow us inna de police cell? And fi waat?

While we wait on the pavement in the cold night air, one police officer each talks to Macy and Tyrone separately. Jerome hangs onto my hand. His palms are sweaty, as are mine, while we pretend we don't see the eyes in passing cars slowing down to see exactly what it is we are guilty of. For we know that we are guilty, until (with difficulty) proven to be innocent. But even then, somehow, we are still guilty. We can all feel it.

They separate Macy and Tyrone and speak to them for some moments while Jerome and I wait. Then it is our turn. We are separated on the street. Jerome led a short distance away by one officer and I am led away by the other. My hands get tighter around my waist as I feel guilt's icy fingers creep up my neck. I swallow, pushing it back down as I try to meet the officer's eyes. He is staring directly into mine, boring into me with an intensity that I find invasive. I can't hold his gaze. He reaches into his back pocket and takes out a little note pad. "Name?"

"My name? I am Maya."

"Just Maya? Do you have a surname?"

"Maya... sir. I'm fifteen." I add in a 'sir' for good measure. Seen it enough times on television, you don't want to get on the wrong side of the police, even if you are in the right. He just looks at me for a moment.

"Where are you going to Maya?"

"We are just going to a Christmas party."

"And do you know the individuals you are travelling with?"

"Yes."

"What are their names?"

"Macy... I am not sure what her surname is, but she is with Tyrone. Tyrone is Jerome's brother, and he is with me."

He writes this all down in his little black notebook. I glance over to Jerome and he has his back to me while the officer is asking him questions too. Macy and Tyrone are waiting on the pavement, apart, as the officers question us.

"And how do you know Jerome?"

"We go to school together."

"What school is that?"

"City Academy."

He notices me flashing Jerome a worried look and attempting to get Tyrone's attention.

"Please keep your attention on me," he says without looking up from his notebook.

My eyes glance towards the floor, embarrassed at having been told off. "To the best of your knowledge, are there any narcotics or illegal firearms in this vehicle?"

I shake my head while Clare screams at him.

Of course, there bloody well isn't! Like you well know! They're just kids! Oh for fuck's sake! More bloody tomfoolfuckery! Again!

He finishes writing in his book, and tells me to wait where I am, while he goes and confers with his colleague. Next, they begin a search of our car.

It takes a good ten minutes as they empty the glove

compartment, feel underneath all the chairs in turn, they open the boot and take out various items, searching for something, before they go back to each other and talk in private.

I am cold. I risk a look at Jerome who is scowling at the officers. They walk over to Tyrone and they talk for a moment before Tyrone waves at me and Jerome to get back into the car. Macy also follows.

As we climb back into our car, the police officers go back to their car, buckle themselves in, and slowly drive away as they watch us settle down.

"What did they want?" Jerome looks at his big brother for answers, but even I can see Tyrone doesn't have any.

"Nothing..." he says, as he starts the engine kissing his teeth, "absolutely nothing."

7

I want to say the party was a blast. And it was, despite teachers being there. They kept a low profile. And I think Mr. Johnson was in a private room drinking with Miss Skelton. Everyone noticed how he came out of the room occasionally, looking redder and redder as the evening went on. But the evening was messed up.

I lie in my bed thinking it all over. I am shaking. Still. And a bit in disbelief that I would've done the things I did and said the things I said. That couldn't have been me. But the alternative sounds crazy and I wonder if I am losing my mind. I mean, not everyone has a raging Clare inside them, do they? And when I think of when she first materialised, I would say it was about a year ago. That was sort of when I became aware of myself. Anything else before that is gone. I managed to piece together bits and pieces from photo albums and talking to family members, etc. You can't exactly hide not remembering your past. Although my problem is that I have too much past. It isn't possible. And yet it is.

The parents even took me to psychiatrists and

therapists, and I have been diagnosed as having a sort of amnesia. But I knew better than to tell anyone about Clare. That would surely make things worse. I had decided to keep her a secret, and I am glad I did. The mother told me that things would settle down once I went back to school. They say 'back', I say I am going there for the first time.

Clare, over time, has become more and more vocal, and I feel less and less like myself. Although even that is hard to describe. I am Maya. I know I am. But I am feeling more like Mary these days. Which I think is progress. The parents don't like to talk about it. Part of me thinks I scare them, but the other half knows they are just worried about what people would think of us. So as long as I act 'normal' they pretend that my 'little episode' of not remembering has vanished and I am 'back to normal'.

And that is fine with me. The evening of that party though has left me scared. It is hard to know who to talk to, and what I can say. I miss Momma. And I miss a Caribbean that I have never been to.

The party was on a boat by the River Thames. Up a newly manicured, grassy bank nestled in some ancient, large trees was a building all lit up. The building is a school, 'St Joseph's School For The Gifted'. The impressive, red brick building reminded me of a castle. All it needed was a moat. But, the party in question was on what looked like an enormous floating hotel, right on the River Thames, hidden in busy London.

Annabel and I danced like fiends as Michael chatted to Saif. He didn't come with Mal as Annabel and I had predicted but he came with Reign... of all people.

Reign was wearing a red, slim-fitting dress over her chubby body. She looked like a forced-ripe plum. Annabel and I took pictures of her when she was dancing with Saif, who was all limbs and arms flailing all over the place. His tangle of black hair was shaking in all directions as Annabel and I watched, trying to snap him in embarrassing moves. Annabel took videos, but I didn't want to use up space on my phone with Saif.

The pièce de résistance though was that Mal actually showed up. She wasn't wearing what Annabel and I had imagined her in. She wasn't wearing anything too interesting actually. It was what she said and what happened on the grounds near the boat that was bothering me.

Mal came along to the party. I'll admit, I'm not being mean or anything, but I was firstly surprised that she could afford it and secondly, that anyone even asked her. As the evening drew on it was clear that no one had asked her. She literally came along on her own. That alone made me give her a bit of credit; that took guts. But she also looked like a bit of a desperado. If I were her, I don't think I would've bothered. But it was later, when I stupidly decided to talk to her, that things kicked off. It was *mostly* her fault, if not all her fault. I should've known better than to go and talk to her.

Michael was getting on my nerves. As he usually does at school. That's the thing about boys, they are immature. Despite being handsome. Here we were at a party and all he could do was mess about with Saif. Anyone would think that he came to the party with him! Annabel had been abandoned by John, and Charlotte was busy with another Year 8 by whom we knew the look of, but no one spoke to. It was Reign that surprised us though. She came to the party and she danced non-stop. And every time I looked over at her in her plum dress, she was laughing, and dancing and sweating... profusely. Her hair even came out of her bun, strands drifting across her face as she was twirled around the dance floor by Andrew, a boy in Year 9. Annabel, after a while, went off with Sophia for a bit and I went outside to get some air. It was there that I saw Mal.

The Ball was just a party. Teachers like to exaggerate. The boat though was impressive. The huge, bobbing, sleek boat's LED lights were glittering in the dark. A pounding baseline vibrated in my chest as we walked up the wooden pathway and out towards the boat that floated in deeper waters. Tickets cost quite a bit but most of the parents don't mind paying it. This Ball is apparently held every year. Of course, I don't remember but the mother came to St Augustine's when she was younger. And talks of it fondly. The Ball in her final year was the one she loved the most. I hardly saw the fact that she was an ex-pupil as positive advertising for the school. She doesn't exactly have a high-flying job. But when I was going back in Year 8, I went along with it.

Mal looked all right. You could even say that she looked a bit pretty. Now I know Mal is ugly, there's no getting away from that, but she looked fairly decent at the Ball. She definitely made the best of what she had. 'Scrubbed up well', as the mother would say.

She wore a pale-yellow dress with white lilies on it. A chiffon material that flowed when she walked. Her freckles danced on her big nose when she spoke - yes, I spoke to her. Her hair was straightened and curled into loose ringlets. Her normally frizzy curls were tamed and were quite long. It fell, dark and smooth, about her shoulders and shone with gold flecks - no doubt they were sprayed in, but it looked okay. It was when I left the boat for a walk around the grounds to gather my thoughts that I saw her.

I had noticed earlier on that Mal was on the dance floor, dancing alone - a braver girl than me. It looked very much like she was having a good time, but now, as she sat outside alone, I wasn't so sure. I walked up to her, my shoes clicking on the cold concrete, the moonlight bathing us in an eerie glow. She sat on the cold grass behind a tree.

There was no way I was going to sit on the floor in my glorious dress, so I walked up to the tree and stood next to her. I didn't think she knew I was there and as I thought about whether I should reveal myself, she spoke.

"Come to gawk have ya?" There was that sneer I had seen so many times before, but somehow there wasn't that sharpness that usually went with it. I said nothing. To be honest, I wasn't sure what to say.

I thought about telling her how nice she looked, but I didn't want to do that. Think there's some part of me that really doesn't like the girl, but there's also a part of me that tells me she's okay. Clare was yelling at me, then telling me what to say, explaining how I should react, but I wasn't listening. I didn't want to encourage her; she had been silent for ages and suddenly here she was again. The best course of action I decided was to pretend that she didn't exist.

Eventually, I broke the silence.

"Who did you come with?" knowing full well she came alone.

"No one."

"No one?" She was silent as she looked out across

the lawn at the side of the school building. At the end of the green was a grassy hedge and beyond that I had guessed there were stone statues and then the car park. The place was reminiscent of The Secret Garden.

Mal sniffed and her breath plumed. She must be cold. I was. I shivered in the moonlight and wondered how my golden hair looked in silvery light. The silence stretched on. And I felt awkward. I should've stayed where I was, with Annabel by the dance floor. But Annabel is Annabel. A twelve-year-old girl and most of the time, although I am thirteen-year-old Mary, I feel like thirty-seven-year-old Maya. Some of the time. Most of the time though, I am somewhere in between. Annabel, although I would never tell her to her face, can be insufferable.

"Why did you bother coming in the first place?" I said. "I mean, didn't you know it would be like this?" Black guilt slid around in my insides. And that made me feel annoyed. I went over to see her and quite frankly, she should be grateful - no one else was really talking to her. And here I was, feeling guilty and trying to... I don't know. Make something up to her? I wasn't sure what though. And there it was again, slick, oily guilt.

And then I hear her sniffing. She started crying. I rolled my eyes, sighed deeply and looked to the deep, black sky.

"Are you crying?" I asked, knowing full well she was. I looked down on her from where I stood.

"No!" That vicious snarl was back again, as well as the defiance in her eyes that shone a little too much as she blinked too much. I screwed up my face and regretted coming over. I almost got my legs to obey the command to walk away - almost.

"Why did you come?" I asked again, genuinely interested by the answer. Mal turned and looked at me. Her sneer was gone, replaced by a deflated face. "I mean, if it was me, I don't think I would bother. If I didn't have any friends."

"Oh, well lucky you do not know how I feel."

I did know how she felt but I certainly wasn't going to let on how unpopular I was before she arrived. And although I didn't remember everything from Year 7, I had the familiar feelings of loneliness: being isolated and pretty much hated by your peers. I didn't need to remember the details to know Annabel, Michael and others regularly called me names and ostracised me from the rest of the kids.

"Hey! It's not my fault!" I sing-song at her, making it sound as though she was completely over-reacting and taking it out on the wrong person. After all, I was there trying to help her and make her feel better. The girl should be grateful, not attack me. It was typical. *Of course it's your fault you fuckin' inbred!* Clare piped up. I began to get angry.

"I thought you were gone," I mutter half to myself, half frustrated that I just didn't seem to get rid of this... whatever Clare was, out of my head.

Mal looked at me and I remembered that she couldn't hear Clare. She must have thought *I* was crazy. But I wasn't crazy. Just getting angry. Perhaps my anger was fuelling Clare, but I was getting tired of all her cussing and her anger. She needed to go.

"It's always hard going to a new school," Mal said whilst suspiciously eyeing me. But instead, all I could see was how Mal was going for the sympathy card. I know all about going to a new school! And this was about something else entirely. I knew what this was about.

"Oh! This has nothing to do with going to a new school and you know it!" I said. But this was what was weird. They were my words. I thought them in my head, formed them with my mouth, released them into the atmosphere, but it was definitely Clare's voice. Anger was bubbling inside me, not tempered in the least by the surprise of hearing Clare, instead it was the opposite. Having Clare in my voice seemed to fuel me. And I felt strong. Powerful. My heart began to thump.

"No. Nothing to do with the school. More to do with the kids." I waited, pretended I didn't know where this was going, but I knew.

"You think I don't know what they think of me?" I waited. Her eyes filled up. "They think I am ugly. They call me aggressive and violent..." she sighed. "In my last school, mum thought it was better to pull me out. Yes, I am half white but I am also black. Mum says the world will treat me as a black woman. I hadn't realised what she meant until, well, I was *shown* what she meant. Kids kept on and on about how me and my mum ate dog poo for dinner. Once, and fair enough, you get angry and it gets dealt with, but again? And again? You just end up getting angry all the time."

"I take it you don't like being black then." I could hear myself. What a stupid thing to say. Of course she doesn't like being black, who would?

"What? Why would I not like being black? That's ridiculous." She tutted at me, and right then, my anger started swirling. She had the cheek to be talking to me like I was an idiot.

"Just because stupid people are rude about something they do not understand, why would I hate what I am? There is nothing to hate. I love my skin and my culture. I love my dad, and my family. And I love our colour. It is who we are. I am not stupid enough to hate myself because some person who has no idea who I am, tells me to!"

Well, of course that made sense to me. More than she knew, but it wasn't that simple.

"You know I should be in Year 9? The bullying last year meant I had to go back a year." I raised one eyebrow in surprise. "My mum is white, my dad is black and I am mixed, but I am still black. And there is nothing wrong with that. As cliché as it sounds, it is other people with the problem, not me. I am not going to hate myself because they hate me. That is stupid. And I am not stupid." Then she gave me a 'look'. My heart skipped a beat and I had to catch my breath. Did she suspect something?

"You don't think I see you pretending? I know you are pretending."

Of course she's fucking pretending! Because people like you sit and do nothing when you should have been HELPING HER! Clare was back in my head. This was the first I had known of her jumping around. I looked inwards, and there she was. Furious, steaming. I swear I could see smoke coming out of her ears.

"Of course, I am pretending too. I pretend they don't upset me, but they do," Mal replied. "But you are also pretending. You think I don't know? You pretend to be this person you present; you pretend to not see when I am bullied and have boys be horrible to me! You just pretend and pretend and pretend! When you could so easily be on my side and help me!"

Well, that shut me up... for a bit. She *knew?* I looked at her, confused. How could she know?

Reaching out a hand I quickly checked my hair to see if I still had my silky 'white girl' hair. Was I still white? Could she see me as Maya? Was I still Mary? To my relief, I was.

"I am not pretending!" My voice squeaked and my face grew hot at the lie.

"YES, YOU ARE!" She yelled a little too loudly, while her face screwed up again, and I realised that that was her hurt face. All the time when her face was scowling or grimacing or snarling, she was really hurt on the inside. She was ugly, yes, but hurt too. When she attacked, and fought, and was ready to spring at someone, she was hurting. I recognised it. I felt it. And it made me even angrier.

"Oh! Stop being so fucking pathetic!" I retorted. "Get a backbone why don't you!" Clare's voice rang out from my mouth. I was shocked. But I didn't stop it.

"Moan, moan, moan, but you don't actually do anything about it do you? It was you who whispered to me on the playground, calling me Bloody Mary... and now you expect me to fucking feel sorry for you?"

Mal's fists balled by her side as I realised that I was

getting her angry. Good. She got me angry! If she is going to behave a certain way, she has to accept the consequences.

"What tomfoolfuckery is this?" I pointed to her rolled up fists. "Ooh you gonna fight me? Come on then! You're pathetic." I spat. "Go on, throw the first punch, I'll give you a free shot."

I pushed my chin forward like I had seen on television. And as I did so, I glanced at Mal to see if she would take the bait. I don't know what I thought I was doing, but at that moment, when I looked at Mal's face, it wasn't her face I was looking at. It was Clare's.

Big, brown, angry eyes were glaring right back at me, and all the bravado I felt moments ago melted away as the cold reality struck me. It was Clare. All of it. And now, as Mal glared at me, it was Clare who was staring me down, in Mal's eyes. And she was livid.

My knees buckled. All my bravery hissed out of me. But before I could back off and make my excuses of not knowing what got into me, Mal shouted, "I tell you who is fuckin' pathetic! Some fuckin' jumped up thirteen-year-old in her mommy's dress, thinking she's all Miss Popular!" And with that she swung her fist at me and it landed square on the jaw that I had stupidly invited her to hit.

To say I saw stars was an understatement. I screamed. And I began to cry. I fell onto the grass clutching my face as Mal stood over me. Her cold, sharp eyes bore into me and without a shadow of a doubt, I knew that wasn't Mal. It was Clare. Her image danced in front of my eyes as I tried to focus. After the amount of times I had wished Clare gone, of how I had ignored and pushed her further and further out into her boat so I couldn't hear her cusses, now I felt her loss, her betrayal. Had she abandoned me and gone to Mal?

"Don't you ever call me pathetic again, you fuckin' inbred. You hear me?" Clare grew in stature and seemed to tower into the night sky. Stars framed her head as she became silhouetted and blended into the black. Her looming shape blocked out the light of the moon and the darkness seemed to flow into her, giving her strength. Tears streamed down my face and I let the silver snot snake to my lips. And as I did, Mal's face changed. It relaxed. And the anger evaporated. Seeing me sobbing on the ground, her form shrunk as she ran off into the darkness.

I felt stupid. And my face hurt. Confused, I looked up into the night sky and wondered what on earth had just happened. Clare jumped out of my body. How was that possible? How was any of it possible? Gingerly, I pulled myself up and examined my dress for grass stains. A cool wind blew, teasing strands of hair tickled my neck. And for a moment, I wondered if my eyes were still blue.

What a fuck-for-all that was! Call that a fight? You really are pathetic, aren't you? Clare was back. I was checking my tights weren't torn when Clare's face flashed up in Mal's. But it couldn't have. Clare is in me, in my head, no one else's. I began to feel angry again.

"What the fuck do you want?" I muttered.

Ooh! Got a bit ballsier! Heat began to rise in my face as I began to make my way back to the boat and it was then that I saw him. Michael. Skulking around the edge of the boat, and round his form I saw puffs of smoke. Typical.

He was the one who picked on me. He was the one

who deserves to be balled out, so instead of going back to the pounding noise of the Ball, I made my way to the figure near the water's edge.

"Oi! Michael!" I saw the cigarette in his hands. Thirteen and smoking. What an arse.

"Oh, hi. Want some?" He offered me a drag. Instead, the anger inside of me rolled up inside towards my throat and exploded in a punch. Michael staggered backwards and dropped his cigarette. The release felt good and I smirked.

"What are you doing you stupid cow!"

"Bloody Mary? What was it you called me?" Spit and blood dribbled down his chin. "I'm not the one who is bloody now, am I?"

Michael looked on, dazed. "Er..."

"Did you think all was forgiven?"

"No!" he said, looking around for someone, anyone who would come to his rescue.

"No, fuckin' Saif is nowhere to be found." I said, balling my fists to thump him again. "Not so cock-sure of yourself, now are you?" I was mad. It blazed out of nowhere and had grown so big inside me that it felt like it was bursting out. Suddenly I didn't care that my face was hurting. Hell, I couldn't even remember why I had let that girl touch me in the first place! Clearly it was a lucky punch. This was who deserved my anger.

And I was enjoying it. Being on the receiving end for so long, it felt good to give some of it back to those who deserved it.

And then suddenly again, I was calm. My stomach flipped at the sudden change of pace. What on earth was happening? Silence surrounded me. And warmth. The ground underneath me was unstable and the light blinded me. But as my eyes got used to the glare, I looked around, shocked to see where I was.

I was surrounded by blue. I stumbled and the small boat I was standing on wobbled, threatening to throw me overboard. I clasped the sides and crouched down low to steady myself. Squinting, I looked into the vast, cloudless sky and saw a tiny blazing, hot sun.

"What?" I whispered to myself incredulously as, eyes wide, I scanned my surroundings. And it was then that it started. Quiet at fast, like a buzzing in the corner of my head. Like white noise.

The buzzing grew and grew. Voices. Overlapping.

Whispering, shouting. Crying. Pleading.

I glanced around. Where was it coming from? But as they grew louder, I saw nothing but warm sunshine and a clear, blue sea.

And there, hanging up in the sky, was a large screen. I watched confused. The screen showed a night's sky, in contrast with the bright, blue sky it was suspended in. On it, was me. Except it wasn't me. I was shouting and swearing and waving my arms around. I could see myself as clear as day. I screamed. Shouted as loud as I could above the cacophony of overlapping voices, as I watched the horror unfold. The voices rose as fast as my panic, shouting and crying. The noise filled my ears. My hands tried to block it out but it was too great. The noise was inside me, around me and below me. And there, deep in the waters, movement caught my eyes. Without knowing what it was, I grew afraid. I didn't want to look, but I had to. I was compelled to. I didn't have a choice.

Tipping myself slightly towards the edge of the boat, I saw the shadows. Dark, humanoid shadows swirling just beneath my flimsy boat. I felt their threat. I could feel their voices vibrating through the waters to the base of the boat and I cried out to myself in fear, to the screen. I yelled as loud as I could, but she couldn't, or wouldn't, hear me. I jumped up again and nearly turned the boat over as it rocked furiously, waving my arms trying to get her attention. It was no good.

It was then that I saw the attack.

They were arguing. I tried to calm myself and sit still, straining to hear through the noise what was being said. I heard her telling him to shut the fuck up. Then, like lightning, Michael was down on the ground. I gasped. He curled up into a ball, and me, no, Clare, in my body, pulled back her foot and kicked him in the ribs, hard.

And although I was a million miles away, although I was a world away, and although my ears were stuffed with screams and cries of voices I did not know, I heard it. And I watched.

I heard the air rush out of his lungs as his face seemed to lose colour. I saw in slow motion him curl into a foetal position, hands cupping his head which curled round to meet his knees. I heard the crack as her foot made contact with his ribs and the 'oooff' sound he made. I screamed. And in a flash, I was back in my body, in the dark, looking at Michael crumpled on the floor. The cool night air doused my hot body. But I just stood, unable to move. My mind went blank as I watched blood seep out of the corner of his mouth.

'Run!' was all I heard ringing in my ears before I took off across the lawn.

The television is still on downstairs and I can hear Mum and Dad moving around. They waited up for me, which normally I would find so embarrassing, but I am grateful. I look at my hands, now I am sitting in the safety of my room. My knuckles are red. I have never punched anyone in my life. Not as Maya or, as far as I know, as Mary. 'This is completely fucked up,' I think. Then suddenly freeze, scanning the words in my head to see if they are mine, or Clare's. Or perhaps they are Maya's.

I had run off across the lawn leaving Michael on the floor and the sound of his retching. I needed to go home. I needed to figure out what was going on. And at the same time, I didn't know what I needed or what I should do. After laying low for a bit, Annabel came and found me. It was time to go. Gratefully I got into the car that was waiting in the car park near where I was hiding, without seeing Michael. Too scared to ask Annabel about him, I listened as she babbled on and on about how good the party was, but Michael's face flashed in my mind and the sound of my foot sinking into his ribs rang in my ears.

Dad is still celebrating the news about his job. They have Indian takeaway downstairs. Dad has curry, he always has curry, and mum always asks for curry chips. I sit on my bed, thinking. What am I supposed to do now? My hand hurts. The only thing I was grateful for was that Clare was silent. I gingerly looked inwards and saw her on the boat. The same little wooden boat I had been sitting in. Her eyes bore into me as anger rolled off her in waves.

A blinking from my phone catches my eye and so I sit up slowly and grab it. Annabel is messaging me on Snapchat. I wonder if she knows about Michael or even the argument with Mal. And I wonder if I should tell her. I don't want to talk to her yet though... I click on Instagram to see what is up there. My heart pounding, I scan the pictures for Michael. Part of me thinks that Annabel had taken pictures of everything that happened, said nothing, and posted them online for me and the rest of the world to find.

My likes have shot up from over two hundred to just under three hundred now. Scrolling through my pictures in my gallery, I quickly delete the ones that are not so favourable of me. Running on autopilot, I edit some of the photos. I smooth up my skin, making it look flawless. I also tan myself a little browner, giving myself a healthy glow. And, (why ever not?) I make my teeth a shade whiter. On some pictures, I add a pea green background tint to make my eyes shine out more. Momentarily, the blue-green water flashes in my mind, and I push it away. Clare bristles.

On others I blur the faces in the background, so I am the only one seen. The pictures might come in useful if I need an alibi. If Mal reports me. Oh God! If Michael reports me! I hadn't thought of that! I could go to jail! How would I explain it? Then the whole world would know I am mad. And the parents would know their therapy didn't work.

My eyes blur over with tears as I try to pretend that nothing happened with Mal and nothing happened with Michael. I was good at pretending. I pushed away the images in my head and ignored my throbbing hand. Once they are all fixed, I upload and wait for the millions of likes I am sure to get.

While I wait, I also look through my photo album on my phone more carefully, and there, in the background of one of the pictures of me and Michael (looking like the perfect couple) and behind us in the corner, is Mal. I hear her cussing in my head, an echo of earlier. And I see my foot in Michael's ribs again. The *woosh* of air from his lips as he curls in a ball. I remind myself that Clare is not real. She cannot come out of my body because she is a figment of my imagination. The lie comforts me somewhat but I still feel slightly panicked. If it wasn't Clare, then... was it me?

She isn't real. I tell myself that again and again. Clare is not real; therefore she cannot want my body and cannot live my life. But as I think the words, I get a sinking feeling that I am wrong, and at that very moment, I feel Clare. And I know. I am right.

I try to forget, to push it away, but it's still there; Clare is still there and suddenly, out of the blue, whilst sitting on my bed, I am fully and completely Maya again, fully grown Maya. Maya whose memory was joined up. Maya who silenced Clare with whisky and antidepressants. Maya who slept soundly in the black. And I remember her hurt, my hurt. Her effort to show people that she was good, and my heart ache when I felt her fail so miserably. She failed so badly that she preferred to sleep. Maya who felt her insides were tied up in a straitjacket. My breath catches as I feel the straps tighten around my chest. My arms suddenly whip across my middle. I feel the straps buckle up tighter and tighter as I struggle to catch my breath. My eyes grow wide and glassy as I collapse sideways on my bed. And then I know. Through the pain and the fear and the anger. I am losing my mind.

I'm sitting on the train on my way to work, another grey day, but it's the last week of term. To say I am tired is an absolute understatement. My eyes burn as I shut them gently and caress my lids with my fingertips. And time stops.

And time jumps. Bunny hops in front of me as I whizz through the Essex countryside, and time flashes forwards and I am teaching and teaching and teaching full speed, my voice rips at a high-pitched falsetto while I run and skip and sashay my way through the day and I walk, I walk, I walk to the station with my Caribbean sway and then time stops. And I am nothing. Black.

And I'm awake, driving my car to God knows where at God knows what time, and I realise that I have lost control. I'm in my car and I don't know what came before or what should be coming after. I'm in my car and I don't know how I got from the train going to work, to being in my car driving down a street that I don't recognise, and I don't know what day it is or what time it is, or where I should be or where I have been or where I am going to, if I am on the right path or if it has been snatched away from me and I am breaking new uncharted ground that is rocky and arduous but will be worth it in the end, or maybe I am just completely and utterly lost in the dark and I am driving, driving, driving; reluctantly forcing myself forwards and onwards.

My memories aren't joining up. I can't remember and I don't have anyone to remember for me. Nothing seems to be making sense as I know I have dropped the threads and there's a pair of scissors that have cut through my memory line. I hold my hands up.

"Okay! I give up! You win!"

You win.

I am on Citalopram coupled with Propranolol. The first will take a while to work, while the second will work immediately. She was right, the doctor that is, and I sleep straight away.

I sleep and I do not dream.

School gets along fine without me. I take Milly to her school and back and I find out what it's like to be a stay-at-home parent for a while. And I lick my wounds.

The points still aren't joining up but I feel that I have left them behind. Like there's a line drawn in the sand. And when I feel the darkness closing in, which is pretty much when I am awake, I go to sleep. My day consists of taking Milly to school, back home and sleep until 3 p.m., then pick Milly up, cook dinner and wait for the other two to arrive. In bed by 9 p.m. and sleep through the night in a dreamless sleep.

I sleep and I do not dream. I sleep and I do not dream. I sleep and I do not dream. Clare screams on but only when I am awake. As I sleep so does she. My memories aren't joining up and my days blend and bend into each other. The silence is warm and fuzzy, and the emptiness doesn't hurt. The best part is when I'm swimming in a lake of black nothingness in a long and dreamless sleep. It is bliss. And I never want to wake up.

I've taken off my white dress and have on my pink, fluffy dressing gown. I don't remember coming around, but the feeling of despair lingers. My golden hair, still shiny from the Christmas Ball, spills over my shoulders - I think it has grown. I stroke it. Its silky-smooth touch comforts me and I reassure myself that I am me. There are no restraints holding me down. I am free.

Dad is watching the news from America. Another protest on Black Lives Matter. I can feel Clare. I don't verbalise it, but I am scared of her. Of myself. *For* myself.

"Black Lives Matter... What utter rubbish!" Dad says. I slowly flip flop in my slippers and perch on the sofa. I'm safer with others around me. Clare wouldn't come out with others around me. I hoped.

The programme talks about the black people being shot for apparently nothing. I distract myself with the television. Dad is watching and shouting comments either at mum or the television. The black people are staging marches and sit-ins. They are complaining about police stop-and-searches. I am reminded of what happened with the police on the way to the Ball. They didn't stop and search us. I don't really think there's a problem with it in this country. And I see Clare on her boat, in the distance, putting her hands over her ears. Black music notes are floating up from her mouth and into the sky. They disappear into the clouds.

I shift on the sofa.

Dad is eating fried chicken and mum asks if I want some. I say no. I continue to watch television.

There are deaths in custody, men and women shot

by police, as well as stop-and-searches... some have filmed it on their phones, others have streamed it on the internet. I wonder how much truth is in the reports and how much is exaggerated. I see the music notes again.

It reminds me of a book I read once, Martin Luther King and the NAACP. I can't remember what that stands for though. Mum comes in with a tray of chicken.

"Of course black lives matter..." Dad says with a mouth full of chicken, "as do white lives; *all* lives matter. If we have a march about it though, we get called racists. Ridiculous." He takes another bite of chicken. I see bits of batter get stuck in the tangle of his moustache.

"You know what all this reminds me of?" he says in between chews. "Black History Month. You hear of that sometimes too. Haven't got White History Month, have we? Ridiculous. One rule for them, and another for the rest of us."

I think of Clare and of Maya and of Michael and of Mal. And I decide to go to my room.

8

January brings with it cold weather and a new term at school. Clare has been quiet. Michael and Mal have said nothing to me and so I have followed their lead and just avoided the whole thing. I take my Maya book back to the library. I've read it enough. Time for a change. I look in the fantasy section and quite fancy something involving magic and dragons. In the end I come away with a Robin Hobb book.

It's break-time and I am out in the playground with the girls. Reign has had a birthday and is now thirteen, whereas I am looking forward to being fifteen. I had my birthday over the Christmas holidays. It didn't feel real. My birthday as Maya feels more like it's true, and I'll be thirty-eight this summer.

Saif and Michael play football and Annabel and I perch on the wooden bench in the playground. It's cold. I think I can sense a frost, or snow, or something coming. I pull my mac around my shoulders a bit tighter.

"So, are you and Michael together now?" Annabel tried to be casual, but I get a feeling she's been wondering since the Ball. I make a mental note to put some pictures of us up together on Instagram.

"Yes, we are," I say, without meeting her eyes and without thinking about how Michael might respond. Especially after what happened. Having a boyfriend is a big deal. I'm older than the others and having a boyfriend will make me better than those little girls. With everything that has happened, I don't want to go back to being where Mal is. Annabel shifts on her seat and I know she is jealous.

"What about you and John?" I ask, knowing full well that there isn't anything going on there. I had found out from Sophia that John only asked her to the Ball as a favour to his parents. They were buying him an electric guitar, or a computer game, or something - I have forgotten the details. The point is it was a pity date. This makes me smile.

"John? No, he's not really my type," she says, while coughing slightly and turning away.

"I heard he was doing it as a favour to his dad who knows your dad. They wanted you to go with someone they knew so you'd be safe?" Annabel was going red and I was enjoying myself. "I'd hate my parents to arrange my social life for me..." Sophie and Reign wander over and join us silently. I stand up and feel myself growing. Surveying the playground, I realise that I want to be the leader of our group. Annabel is on her way out. With this knowledge, I turn and look at her. She has shrunk a bit but still has a defiant look in her eyes. And I think to myself how easy that was. Game on.

Michael is playing football with Saif and I decided to go and speak to my 'boyfriend'. I leave the girls and feel their eyes following me. As I do, I remember that I will have to update my wardrobe. If I am going to be better, I will have to accessorise correctly.

My blonde hair swishes as I walk over to Michael. His dark hair is sculpted to one side and his brown eyes look watery in the cold as his breath plumes. He sees me coming. I don't know what I am going to say to him. Annabel and the girls are watching from the bench, but luckily cannot hear what I am saying.

"Did you get it back or not?" Michael is chatting to Saif in between kicks at the wall. I stand next to him. From where they girls are, if they glance over, it looks like we are talking.

"Yeah, I got it back." Saif kicks the ball and it thuds on the brick wall.

"And? Did Ugly take it?"

"I reckon so. I just found it stuffed in the corner of my locker."

"Money still in there?" Michael kicks the ball back onto the wall. It bounces hard and Saif runs to meet it with his foot.

"Money's still there, yeah. No one else it can be mate."

"It could be anyone really..." I chance a comment and they turn around to look at me. I search Michael's face for any clue as to how he feels, but there is none. He just notices me, then turns away again. I wonder if his stomach is still sore and what excuse he has given for the bruise on his face. I decide not to say anything in front of Saif. I swish my blonde hair and stand closer, hoping he can smell my perfume. Saif looks over at me and frowns. I just ignore him.

Thinking about the Ball, I think there are pictures on my phone of Michael and I. Didn't Dad take a picture of us as we left? I don't remember but will check. Michael carries on playing with Saif totally ignoring me.

It's nearly time for the end-of-break bell and so I look back to the wooden bench outside my classroom, and there sitting on it is Mal.

My stomach lurches as I think about our last conversation. I scowl to myself at the awkward position I have found myself in. Mal still has those ugly cornrows in her hair that she undoubtedly thinks are pretty. The shampoo advert flashes in my mind with the girl that has perfect, shiny, blonde hair. Mal looks as if she slept in the cornrows as they are a bit crumpled at the bottom and has strands escaping from in between the tight rows and I don't understand how she can prefer her hair to hair like mine. Everyone would agree, mine is better.

I walk passed and ignore her. A bit further away from her are my group of girls. Mal doesn't look up.

When I get home from school Dad isn't there. I know he isn't because of what happened last week. Chucking my bag on the floor, I go into the living room. Bella is bounding at my feet and sniffing around in my pockets for sweets. I don't have any. I flop into the chair and switch on the television. More news about Brexit and whether we should have done more negotiating before triggering Article 51 or something. Boring stuff that isn't anything to do with me. I leave the television on and go up to my room, flicking through my phone for a picture of me and Michael at the Ball. It does seem quite a while away now that I think about it. Dad has since got a job. He started his first day last week when it happened.

I had got home from school and Dad wasn't there. It was the first time in ages that he's not been there and it felt weird. Mum says it isn't what he is used to but it's a job all the same. Dad was dressed up all smart the night before, trying out his new clothes that mum bought. He was wearing a grey suit - must be an office job.

Mum was cooking dinner, which I was glad about because I was quite hungry. Curry chips. We've not had that before - homemade ones that is. It is usually ordered from the takeaway, but mum says she could easily make it herself - so she did.

It was at the dinner table that it happened. We didn't eat dinner until Dad came home from work. He isn't very detailed on the details, but he's happy and we are getting money in so if I'm honest, I don't really care. For once we are eating dinner in the dining room. And that's when it happens.

Dad clutches his chest and says he can't breathe. His face goes this weird purple colour. And I just watch. Like I am watching a programme or something. And I think that maybe I am getting desensitised to all this violence. Or maybe it just all doesn't really seem real. He is huffing and puffing and his moustache is twitching, and his eyes are bulging and his veins are popping out of his temples. Mum rushes to his side. I just sit there. It's when mum screams at me to call 999 that I spring out of my seat and rush to my mobile. Dad's face is a deep shade of purple now, a bit brown by the time the ambulance crew get here, and mum is trying not to cry. We both go in the ambulance with him.

It isn't until much later that we realise that he's had a heart attack - and I had thought he had choked on one of mum's home-made curried chips, which didn't taste too bad actually. The shocker came later when Dad got a visit from his boss. Made me wonder just exactly who dad was working for.

A Mr Kokas came in at visiting time. Mum and I nearly fell off our chairs and Dad looked sheepish.

Mr Kokas hadn't been Dad's boss for a long time but still came to see him in hospital. Dad had worked one day. Not enough to be able to apply for sick leave but Mr Kokas said they would figure something out. He was really nice.

He handed mum a bowl that was covered up with a glass lid.

"Kaputsa," he said. "I tried to bring something healthy; this is what my wife came up with." He chuckled like there was a joke but we didn't get it.

His accent was pretty good. I never would have guessed he was foreign. He just looked normal. It did remind me of Dad though and wanting to be out of the European Union because of the too many foreigners being here draining the system. And here was one who was a successful businessman, employing a good honest British person and I wonder if he employed his own people too.

I wrinkle my nose at his gift. I'm not fond of cabbage and this dish smells funny.

I wrinkle my nose at dinner. I've lost my appetite. For some reason when I cook it, it doesn't taste as good as when someone else does it. Instead I have a cup of tea and I slosh some whisky for good measure. It's becoming a habit - I know it is, but I can't deal with Clare at the moment. Besides, she likes whisky.

The kids are in their rooms. That's teenagers for you. So I cook dinner and take my medication while I'm at it. Slosh in a bit of whisky in a cup of tea. I know I'm making a habit of it, but I can't deal with Clare right now.

So I just shove oven chips into the oven and some battered fish. Marcia likes battered fish. It's five o'clock in the afternoon and the kids are in their bedrooms - teenagers - except for Milly. I wonder what she is doing but to be honest, I like the quiet, so I leave her alone.

Time speeds along, or it is really slow. My memories are still not joining up. I forget if I am making breakfast or dinner. Within what feels like minutes, the oven is beeping and I dish up the dinner. My stomach lurches at the thought of chips so I flick the kettle on for a cup of tea. I slosh in a bit of whisky. It's becoming a habit - I know it is, but I can't deal with Clare right now - besides, she likes it. I take my medication. I've lost my appetite. Perhaps it has crawled into bed for some relief - my warm, fluffy bed that constantly calls me. I am so very tired all the time but it's such a relief to sleep. To sleep and not dream.

I call the kids to eat. They come slowly. Marcia takes her plate off up to her room. Milly sits at the table, and the other doesn't materialise. I leave hers in the oven. I wrinkle my nose at the fish - I've lost my appetite.

Milly sits at the table. I turn the television on for her so she can watch SpongeBob while she eats. The noisy, irritating laughter on the television irritates my head. I try to ignore it.

Remembering what I did yesterday is difficult. My memories don't join up and my head is hurting. Marcia brings in her finished plate and puts it in the sink. The clicking noise hurts my head as I realise the dishes have built up. I should wash up. I need to wash up.

Hauling myself into the kitchen, I stand by the

sink. The clock face on the windowsill stares at me; 10 a.m. Shouldn't the children be at school? I blink. My head hurts. I flick on the kettle and make myself a cup of tea, sloshing in some whisky for good measure. I can't deal with Clare today, besides, she likes it. While I'm at it, I take my medication, as well as some Ibuprofen. My head hurts.

My eyes are hurting too as I realise that I need to sleep. Leaving the dishes, I go to my room and lie down. It's constantly dark in here. The heavy curtains block out the light. No need to change, I am already in my nightshirt. I gulp the hot tea. It stings the sides on the way down. I make a point of plaiting my locks into a nice, neat plait down my back. I take my time. I like my shells. I think my hair is pretty, no matter what anyone else says.

Climbing into bed, I realise that perhaps I should have got a bit more whisky - keep Clare quiet, but that thought isn't finished as I close my eyes and drift into a deep, long, clasping, black sleep - bliss. And I think to myself that I might stay here.

9

I lie on my bed in my room. The house is still. As I look over at the bedside clock, I see that it is only just after 7 a.m. Clare is quiet. That is weird. She is normally screaming in my ear about something or other. I have been watching her and I am sure that she is up to something. It is too quiet. I look inwards and I see her.

Muttering on that boat. She has sails now which catch a little wind. She is sailing out further and further into the surrounding blue. I think of the deep waters and what was below the surface and I shiver as I remember the shadows. The ones that yawned hungrily from the depths, stretching out towards the boat. I did not know what they were, but they scared me. I could feel them. It was as if a thousand souls were whispering in my ears, suffocatingly close. I shut my eyes and I hear them again, whispering, muttering curses. I push them away and think of nicer things.

It is after the Christmas holidays. What happened with Michael has seemed to have blown over. He mostly leaves me alone now and I him. Although I have hidden the fact that he is not my boyfriend.

Annabel knows I lied but I told the others that we are still together. They will never guess. I need to find a replacement before I find a way to announce that I dumped him. And I need to find a way to keep Annabel from using what she knows against me. Got to keep up with the playground politics.

I don't think the girls are suspicious, but Michael is now wary of me, which I find strangely enjoyable. I remind myself that it wasn't me who kicked him. It wasn't me who drew blood. And if he wasn't such a bully, it never would have happened. There's no way he will tell people that he had his arse handed to him by a girl. It isn't my fault he was so horrible and there is no way I should feel guilty. I expect Clare to start yelling at that, but I listen, and she is still quiet. I feel uneasy.

Mal is a different matter though. Annabel continues to torment her, and she continues to fight. I avoid it all. Perhaps that is why Clare is quiet but I am not sure. After some thinking, once I had calmed down about what happened on the night of the Ball, I guessed that it is anger that fuels Clare. But why she is so angry I don't know; she lives off it. It's like her chocolate or something, or her cigarettes. She's addicted to it. It feeds her.

And that place where she stays on the boat? It's the whispering voices that are so loud, that causes her to yell all the time. It's a wonder they don't drive her mad. But then I think to myself that Clare is a part of me, and by mere definition of having a voice inside my head that seems to think independently of me proves that I am mad. Clare can't be mad because she is me and I know that she is me. If I didn't, then that would prove that I am mad. I frown. My head hurts. That can't be right. I am not her. I am *not* her.

And then there is Dad. I remind myself that he is not Papa. Dad is in hospital and alive. There is no need to be terribly upset but it is understandable if I am a little upset. But he is not Papa, I repeat, and I think to myself how everything is changing.

I had woken up in a sweat. The sun was creeping into my bedroom. Nowhere near the heat of the sun from my dream. And it was a dream. That is what I tell myself. That is what my mum would say if she came into my room after hearing my cries. Mop my brow and shush me back to sleep. She would tell me that it is just a dream. Nothing but a bad dream.

The heat from the sun was beating down on me as I curled up in that little, wooden boat, bobbing on an endless, blue sea. The white noise of the whisperers stuffed me full. I felt dehydrated and bloated as I squinted and looked up at the sky to see the enormous screen suspended in blue. Blinking, I watched. There she was. Her. Me. Blue-eyed Mary. I knew what I didn't need to see and my heart wept. I didn't want to reach up and touch my hair, but my hand did it instinctively. My hair was rough to the touch. Singed by the sun. The black twists felt dry and brittle. I knew it needed deep conditioning. I looked at my large, adult hands. They were hers. Mine. I was Maya.

It's hard to explain how I felt. My heart sank at the thought of being what others despised - what I had come to despise. But it felt familiar. I felt relieved that what I continually dreaded happening had finally happened. But then, I also felt desperately disappointed. How could I end up here? I wanted to go home, to my bed, to my dog and the mum and dad that loved me.

I pulled myself up. My mouth was caked dry. Peering over the edge of the boat, the first thing I saw was my reflection. Maya's tired, sad eyes looked back. They were big, round and empty. Sort of stretched too far into their sockets so they looked haunted. Her lips were swollen. Dried spit crusted at the corner of her split mouth. Gingerly I licked them and winced at the sharp sting. The thick tongue scraped the roof of my mouth like sandpaper. I tried to wake up, thinking it was a dream, but couldn't. I screamed out in desperation and fear. And although I was screaming with every ounce of my being, there was no noise. It was as if someone clicked mute on the remote control. I was muted. This whole world was muted and I was helpless as I watched the floating screen.

Something had happened. I could feel it. I saw Mary living my life. She was arguing with someone. Her hands were animated, her blue eyes bulging and her brow creased. Momma's brow. But it was more than that. It was Clare.

As I sat on my bed, I thought. Were these dreams or memories that I pushed away? I wasn't sure. I wasn't sure of anything anymore except that I knew I was in my room. I was lying in my bed. When I had awoken, I was so thankful to be home. I could hear the dog snuffling in her sleep under my bed. It was the early hours of Saturday morning and I had been asleep and probably dreaming. I am Mary. I am Mary. I repeat it to myself again and again to remind myself who I am. I am Mary.

It was then that I felt the grumblings of Clare. Finally. For the first time, I feel some kind of comfort at her being back.

I climb out of bed, slip my feet into my soft, light, pink, slip-on slippers and stand.

Bella wakes up and pulls herself out from under my bed. I can hear Mum is up. She is probably getting coffee. I imagine she finds it difficult to sleep without Dad. Bella scratches her belly with her back legs. I bend down and give her an affectionate rub on her head. She yawns and waddles slowly out of my room and goes downstairs in search of food. Pulling my dressing gown around my body, I flip flop my way downstairs and to the kitchen.

"Coffee?" she says as I enter the kitchen. It is quiet without Dad. I nod. Mum doesn't usually offer me coffee. I can see she has been crying. "How is Dad?" I ask, afraid of the answer and that fear surprises me. I care about him. Well, of course I do. He is my dad. He isn't Papa but he is still my dad and I don't want him to die. I can feel hot tears prick behind my eyes as I come to that realisation. He's my dad.

"I haven't called the hospital yet," she says. She slurps on hot coffee and stares ahead. We stand in silence and I awkwardly shuffle. I feel Clare and it reminds me that this is my family now. If the mother cannot be strong, I will have to. I walk over and pull Mum into a hug. She is stiff but I keep holding her. 'This is what a good daughter does,' I tell myself. I can feel, rather than hear, Clare cussing. I kiss my teeth. The noise doesn't sound right in this house, in this kitchen, in this moment. Mum doesn't seem to notice. I let her go. Her eyes still glazed over; she sips the coffee she still holds in her right hand. I decide to go upstairs and get ready. We should go and visit him at least.

As I walk up the stairs, I can hear the cusses from Clare get louder and louder. 'Who do you think you are? You think you can just pretend us away? Think you are this little, white girl? Hell no! You are as black as they come!'

I ignore her and hope she goes away. And I must admit, I feel slightly foolish for missing her loud, vulgar language. I look inward and see Clare standing on the wobbling boat and shouting at me. I silently remind myself again. I am Mary.

The hell you are!

And as if to confirm it to myself, when I enter my bedroom, I look into the full-length mirror. My blonde hair lies softly on my shoulders. And my blue eyes stare back at me. I step closer to the mirror and look deep into my eyes. Yes, they are blue. Clear like the Caribbean sky. Or sea. And there are flecks of green. I am Mary.

You are Maya you dyam fool!

"I am only thirteen."

Er... more like thirty-six.

"I am Mary, I am Mary, I am Mary!" I say my name louder and louder as the noise from that other place fills my ears. And I become afraid. I can feel the nightmare from last night, the voices, the boat, the heat, all on the edge of my consciousness. All waiting like some towering, giant wave getting ready to engulf me. I tremble. I don't know what to do so I shout my name louder. "Mary! I am MARY!" My voice falters at first but then it cracks and breaks and sounds stronger; deeper. Surer. And the louder I shout, the more I can hear that my voice is not my own. It is changing, warping into something else. And I don't sound thirteen anymore. I am sounding older.

Bella has found her way into my room and although I cannot see her, I can hear her barking. I sob as my lips form my name again and again and I hold my head in my hands attempting to block my ears from the noise that was filling my head. "Mary, Mary. I am Mary." By the third Mary, I know. I sound like me. The old me. I sound like Maya. I don't want to believe it and yet my heart thunders the truth out to my head: I am Maya.

Bella stands at my bedroom door as she continually barks. Her distress shows. She moves closer to my legs and looks into the mirror at my reflection as a low growl rips through her throat. I peer into the mirror. I look passed my screwed-up baby face, look passed the tears and the fear in my eyes and look deep into the blue. And it isn't Mary I see looking back at me, but Maya.

I see her clearly. In her beige straitjacket with the tight, black buckles strapping her arms to her form as she writhes to get free. Her black hair, twisted like wires, stand out from her head. Electricity sparks between the twists as blue crackles and flashes, lighting up the darkness where she is incarcerated. Her bloodshot eyes bulge. Her mouth wide, showing her fat tongue as spittle flies and she rages. She screams, shaking in fury and spitting curses. Threats of murder. Of ripping my throat out. Of plunging her fist into my heart. Of gouging out the blue of my eyes. Of watching my hot, red blood run as she laughs. Her wild eyes hold me in fear as she emerges out of the darkness and slowly comes into full view. And I see her clearly. And she is me.

Suddenly everything is clear. I glance at Clare, still in the boat but sitting calmly and waiting. What is she waiting for? I look back at Maya who was still screaming, still tied up in her straitjacket, but is now close to me. So close I could reach out and touch her! So close I feel her warm breath on my face. I flinch as her foamy spit lands on my cheek as she roars in fury. And I realise.

Mary is just a little, white girl. They want full control. Both Clare and Maya. And it is then that I realise they are in it together. They are going to kill me. That much I do know. This knowledge as it flashes through my mind, also flashes through theirs. They know that I know and Maya throws her head back and laughs. Her wild eyes glare down at me from a height as I shrink in her presence. And as she does, the voices from that other place fill my ears completely, screaming and laughing and crying so loud that they fill my whole being. I cannot think. I cannot see. I cannot breathe.

My hand shakes. I think of the mum downstairs and my life flashes. I think of school, the Essex train. Of frosty English mornings and the commuters. I think of the dad, the dog and of Annabel. I think of Michael and even Mal. I think of the Ball, of the playground and of my hair. I see in my mind's eyes, my blue eyes flecked with green. I see my ski slope nose and my freckles. And I want to keep them. I want to keep them all. This is *my* life. I am Mary. I *am*

Mary. I have blonde hair scraped into a high ponytail that swishes back and forth as I walk - and I deliberately swish it. I am Mary. I have eyes that are a sky-blue colour, flecked with an emerald green. I am Mary.

And with that realisation I see a hairbrush on my dressing table from the reflection in the mirror. Maya sees my gaze falter and knows what I am thinking. Like lightning an idea comes to mind, and as soon as it does I know it flashes in their minds too. But I am too fast. I whip round, grab the brush and hurl it in the mirror, smashing it to pieces. Bella runs out of the room. The noise screams in my head and overpowers the voices from that place and I fall back, covering my face as mirror glass shatters and smashes to the floor. And I am left in darkness.

And in my room, the broken glass is strewn all over the carpet. And I am in the void. The mute button is on. Silence is stuffed in my ears like cotton wool. I am blind. I feel a breeze that blows cool in the dark. I think it ruffles my hair. I wait. And breathe.

From where I am in the black, I see a shard of mirror come into view, large and flat. Its surface

shimmers like a black ocean, hinting at an
unimaginable depth. I watch as the silent, black
surface, still at first, ripples. The ripples give way to a
hand that pushes up through the black, pushes up
through the mirror. The hand is followed by an arm
then a shoulder. The sliver of mirror stretches to
allow the shape to haul itself up and out of the
darkness. Brown, strong legs finally scramble through
the mirror as the figure stands tall. Her eyes find mine
as I watch on in horror. Her bare feet crunch on the
broken glass as she gets closer to me, now trapped on
the other side of the mirror. In darkness. She
crouches, picks up a slither of mirror and stares
through it at me. Her huge, brown eyes glare
triumphantly, looking down as I realise where I am. I
watch as the tall, brown figure of Maya morphs and
changes. The black twists slop together and flow as if
underwater. They transform from black to glittering
gold. Her skin changes from brown to creamy white
and her body changes from a grown woman to a child
of fourteen. She is naked. I watch as she transforms
into me. The wardrobe door is open. She reaches in a
hand and takes out a dressing gown that was folded

up and placed neatly in a drawer. I watch as she looks at the gown as if for the first time. She strokes it. Pulls it to her face and breathes it in, and then slowly she wraps it around her body and hugs herself. I cry out in the muted silence, as she turns her back, walks away and does not think of me.

I am small. I am insignificant and I am floating in the dark. I'm in a little, wooden boat on a vast, black ocean that stretches for miles and miles in every direction. And I am alone.

It's a time to start looking forward and not backward. I'm looking forward to Year 9 and being fourteen. Surprisingly, I am still bigger than everyone else and I love it. I continue to grow. Michael and I are known as the golden couple, even though I'm the one with golden hair. I know it is stupid and that he hates me now. We are not together but I haven't set people right and neither has he. It's convenient to let them believe what they want to believe. Gold has become sort of my trademark colour. I have covered most of my backgrounds on Instagram with gold, apart from the ones with close-ups of my face. Most of the photos were taken before Christmas when my eyes were blue. So those backgrounds are turquoise. They bring out my eyes.

The playground is getting that little bit lighter in the morning. At the moment, I am early and as I sit on the bench, I decide to read my book. In the dark of my bag, I see the spine of a Robin Hobb book that I had borrowed but didn't get time to read. Blue- green dragon's eyes stare up at me from the dim of my bag and remind me of someone I used to know. They sparkle and glitter a golden colour which looks pretty. I smile.

Looking around the playground, it's then that I see Mal. I can hear her raised voice, again. Glancing over at her, I see that her head is moving animatedly and although I can't hear it, I know her beads are tinkling. Her hair has grown. Long, brown plaits now brush against her shoulders. I can see from where I am that she is angry - again. That her fists are rolled up into balls - again, that she is poised like some kind of animal, a tiger perhaps or a cobra. Yes, cobra would be more apt, like she is spitting poison from her mouth - again. And I think to myself how some things will never change.

She's having a row. Someone, I can't see who, is having a go and I wonder what she has done this time. Saif got his money back, but I can see him, as well as Michael, giving another boy some support as he challenges her about something. The one girl that needs four or so boys to make it a fair fight. Uh oh... I can see someone has said something really bad to upset her. She's reeling. I can see her mouth doing a large, black 'O'.

Oh my God! What kind of Tomfoolfuckery is this! I don't hear the words too clearly but I see them float out of her mouth in Times New Roman, black, bold letters and I think I can see a tiny figure riding on one of the O's - maybe she's ye-hawing... I don't know.

Mal nearly punches one of the boys but backs down a bit as the four boys crowd her more. I turn my attention to the book in my bag.

The dragon's eyes twinkle up at me and I smile a little - so pretty. I imagine myself riding a beautiful, golden dragon into a clear, blue sky. The dragon hide glittering like magic, matching my golden, sparkly hair that flows out of me like a river, and my eyes blend into the blue of the sky.

I have forgotten about our conversation under the tree. I have forgotten seeing her hunched up and crying. I have forgotten feeling sorry for her and I concentrate on what I see.

She's angry and aggressive all the time. It's a wonder how she doesn't get bored of it all. I get bored of watching it. Her lips are still big and fleshy and fat like caterpillars. Her eyes are still sunken into her face, still small, beady and distrustful, and she still frowns all the time giving herself a permanent crease on her forehead, like her brow is broken in two. I wrinkle my nose... she's so ugly that I have to turn away. And I forget her. I forget them all.

Clare is gone. I sent her where I thought she would be best placed. Somewhere she was needed. If I close my eyes, I can imagine where she is, what she is doing and I hope she finds what she is looking for. I've not forgotten Maya. How could I? But I am Mary. Always have been, always will be.

My blonde hair is golden and flows down my back like a glorious river of riches. And my eyes... my eyes are beautiful. They are a rich, chestnut, golden brown.

Epilogue

It is the day of the funeral. I am in my room. Mum had my mirror fixed. I still like a full-length mirror on my wooden wardrobe. I can hear the people chattering downstairs. Sounds like a bit of a crowd. Mum is playing some soft classical music.

Dad was buried in the local cemetery. The service was good. I managed to cry a bit, even though I don't really know him that much... I imagined what it would be like if it was Papa. But it wasn't Papa. Dad had a heart attack. And it looked like he was getting better. He was planning on going back to work for Mr Kokas. Mum was doing a fairly decent job of looking after him. Things were going well as they were ignoring me and the problems that came with me. I'm guessing that I behave more like my age now, a woman in her thirties, but I remind myself that I have just turned fourteen. I keep up with the ridiculous gossip from school and I work on just living my life and being a good student. Maybe this time, I can ace school and manage to do something brilliant with my life. Maybe this time, I will be allowed. Maybe this time, the path will be clear for me and all I have to do is work hard and I can achieve. I can be anything I want to be.

As I think this, I smile at my reflection. I pick up the brush and roll it around in my palm. I am glad it didn't break. It is only plastic but some things are just built to last. I brush my hair, close my eyes and listen to the sound it makes as it glides effortlessly through my silky, blonde hair.

When I am ready, I go downstairs to the crowd of people. Bella lies under the dining room table. She doesn't like me much these days. At first, she would bark and growl at me whenever I was around. That confuses Mum. Now though, we seem to have found an uneasy truce. We basically avoid each other.

Some people are in our living room, others are milling around in the kitchen. Mum is talking quietly in a corner to a woman I do not recognise. I clear my throat and step into the living room. There I see someone I don't recognise but know - Mr Kokas. Dad's boss.

"Mary." He approached me with a woman by his side. They both smile sympathetically at me, to which

I slightly dip my head to look sorrowful but not too much. "This is my wife, Lena." Lena smiles at me. "I am so sorry about your father, Mary," he continues. "Although I did not know him for very long, I know that he was keen to get back to work. He was an honest man and from what I saw, was a loving and kind father." I nodded my head, unsure of what to say. Ideally, my mum should come now and rescue me. After all, I was a fourteen-year-old child. But the mother was still in the corner, talking quietly.

"That must be your mother?" Lena smiled as her gaze had followed my eyes. I nodded. She smiled again. "You have the same beautiful, blonde hair." That comment made me blush. I felt the heat rise in my neck and rush to my cheeks. Of course, that was where the blonde hair came from. It had to come from somewhere. Just like how I had my big, brown eyes from Mama, and I guess my big hands from Papa. The blonde hair is from the mum.

"Apart from the eyes," Mr Kokas chimed in. "When I look at you Mary, to me it is very clear where you belong. You may well have your mother's blonde hair, but it is your father's brown eyes that you have. That is without a doubt."

I looked up at him with my large, brown, innocent eyes and smiled.

About the Author

The author, Cheryl Diane Parkinson, is a fiction and non-fiction writer born in Plaistow, East London on the 3rd November 1976. She grew up in East London and attended an Ursuline Convent school for girls. She is a British author primarily concerned with black representation and equality for all. Cheryl Diane Parkinson has a BA with Honours in English Literature and American Studies, an MA in Colonial and Post-Colonial Literature in English (taught by Professor David Dabydeen at Warwick University) and a PhD in Creative Writing from Birmingham University (part of the Russell Group). She is a teacher of English Literature and Language at GCSE and A Level and has taught in Coventry and London as well as Cambridgeshire. After the birth of her fourth child, she relocated from Hertfordshire to Norfolk where she currently resides with her four children, partner Zach and mother Monica.

AUTHOR ACKNOWLEDGEMENTS

I would like to thank my mother, Monica, for her continual support and her sheer pride in all I do. I would especially like to thank her for always reminding me how my late father, Ansurd Parkinson, would've been just as proud of me as she is. Thank you Mum.

I would also like to mention my siblings: Angela, Jacquie and Kevin. Thank you for the continual discussions and feedback for Maya and your ceaseless patience.

Thank you for accepting the shared documents with the 'this is the final, final, FINAL draft' messages of more writing for you to read! Thank you to my daughter, Jessica, who did not complain when I printed up my manuscript for her to give detailed written feedback for the millionth time.

Thank you Jessie Bessie for all your comments and questions that help me clarify characters and situations. And for always being interested in what I write.

Thank you to Amelia who sat and listened as I read her chapter after chapter. Her excitement and boundless enthusiasm continues to keep me going.

And thank you to my partner, Zach, for his patience, pride and quiet support in what I do. I appreciate it.

Finally, I would like to mention my grandfather, Thaddeus Parkinson, whom I think of often but never met. Grandad, I hope you would've been proud.

PUBLISHER ACKNOWLEDGEMENTS

The publishers and authors would like to thank
Russell Spencer, Matt Vidler, Susan Woodard,
Leonard West, Lianne Bailey-Woodward and Laura
Jayne Humphrey for their work, without which this
book would not have been possible.

The Publisher would also like to send a special
acknowledgement to Kudzaishe Chiriseri.

ABOUT THE PUBLISHER

L.R. Price Publications is dedicated to publishing books by unknown authors.

We use a mixture of both traditional and modern publishing options, to bring our authors' words to the wider world.

We print, publish, distribute and market books in a variety of formats including paper and hardback, electronic books, digital audiobooks and online.

If you are an author interested in getting your book published, or a book retailer interested in selling our books, please contact us.

www.lrpricepublications.com

L.R. Price Publications Ltd, 27 Old Gloucester Street, London, WC1N 3AX.

020 3051 9572

publishing@lrprice.com

Maya

Printed in Great Britain
by Amazon

83626788R00111